The System
- A Detroit Story -

JOHN SILVER

DEDICATION

For Barb and my family.

Copyright(c) 2011 by John Silver

For updates, previews of other books and projects, behind the scene notes and photos visit http://johnsilverbooks.com.

JohnSilverBooks

ISBN 978-0-578-11036-3

CHAPTER 1

Chris, Clarence and Zippy Boost Escalades

The beater cop surplus Crown Victoria pulled behind the car hauler carrying three Escalades, two black and one white. Chris Wolfe rode shotgun and Clarence Russell drove. The Escalades, not new but off lease and fresh out of auction were easier to boost and harder to trace. Carried by a Mom and Pop hauler- good intel on this one. Chris took a last drag of his cigarette and flicked it out the window. He reached down to the seat and put the cop gumball on the dashboard.

Clarence adjusted the windshield wipers against the intermittent rain. Several times. Chris looked at him and didn't say anything, knowing it was just one of the many things Clarence did to get his mind tuned for the boost.

They rolled over a pothole and the old Crown Vic took it without complaining. Chris and Clarence bounced in their seats.

"Gonna miss this ride," said Clarence.

"Not me," said Chris. "Frame's bent and it stinks. Has that auto parts store smell. I hate it." He looked out the window, scanning the area. "Worst part is, you still smell it, even when you're gone. Stays in your nose."

Chris studied the hauler's hydraulic loader. Old school and simple, but easy to get your fingers pinched, even sheared off. Saw it happen once. He rubbed his eyes, watery from the Vic's rubber and stale oil odor.

"One more year, man," said Chris. "One more year…"

The car's odor was making him sick. He scanned the area again, wet and dull shades of gray. One more year, maybe a little less and he'd have enough cash squirreled away for the TradeWind. Docked and waiting for him, bobbing white and pristine in a little marina just south of Miami.

Right now, he had to push it out of his mind and focus.

Risky, using the gumball on Northbound I-75, but it was late, raining, and Chris figured the odds about 200 to 1 that a State Trooper would roll by this time of night, let alone a Hamtramck cop. Hamtown. Just two cruisers in the entire city, four cops on the road at any given time, nine times out of ten busy responding to bar fights. No worries there.

A DPD squad car passed on the other side of the freeway, no flashers and siren, but moving, *fast*. Chris watched it pass and figured it going about ninety, ninety eight miles an hour.

He looked at Clarence and said, "hit it." Out of habit Chris felt for the Glock 9mm in his jacket pocket and scanned the freeway one more time front, back, and side to side.

"Alright, man," said Clarence, pulling his gray hoodie over his head. He reminded Chris of a young Mohammed Ali ready to enter the ring. Only meaner, a true black panther.

Chris plugged the gumball cable into the cigarette lighter and it instantly rotated and flashed red. This was it- crossing the line, moment of truth, point of no return, whatever it was called. He always had the same feeling, starting in his legs, a tickling sensation that didn't last long.

…just stick to the system…

Clarence flicked the brights on and off then pulled along side the hauler. Chris motioned for the driver to pull over on the oncoming ramp to Holbrook. Even in the darkness Chris clearly made out the perplexed "who me?" look on the driver's face. The driver looked down at him, confused. Chris saw it before, the "are you guys really cops?" look.

He could pass for an undercover cop. Short black leather jacket, black knit sock cap, black t-shirt and jeans, lace up leather boots and two days worth of stubble. Everything cop except the thin leather driving gloves with sticky palms.

The hauler pulled onto the off ramp and drove all the way over to the curb of the intersection of the Chrysler service drive and Holbrook, in view of the stark tan concrete and green glass offices of American Axle. Perfect. The driver stopped, engaged the air brakes and kept the engine running.

Clarence stopped behind the hauler, unplugged the gumball and said, "I got your back."

Chris jumped out, sprinted to the hauler and leapt up to the driver side door. Glock in hand he motioned to the driver to roll down the window.

The bristle faced driver jerked back at the sight of the gun.

"Unlock the other door," said Chris, pointing the gun at the driver's face. "Don't try anything stupid or I *will* shoot you."

The overweight driver, wearing blue striped work overalls that were nearly bursting at the seams moved his entire body as he leaned over and pulled the handle of the passenger side door. Sometimes these old dudes carried guns and jumped at the chance to use them. Sometimes they were gentle as small children. Chris slipped around the front of the hauler, never taking his eyes or the gun off the driver and jumped into the cab.

"Drive," he said, pointing the gun at the driver's ribs.

"Where?" said the driver. His hands gripped the steering wheel.

"Turn right on Holbrook. You got a gun?"

"No," said the driver.

He put the shifter into first gear and the hauler lurched forward, belching black diesel exhaust. He slipped through the rest of the gears and picked up speed. Clarence followed close behind.

Chris looked around the cab. "Where are the keys?"

"Buyer wanted the keys sent separately," said the driver.

"You gotta be shittin' me," said Chris, pushing the Glock into the driver's side. "Where are they?"

"They aren't here. Honest. Look for yourself," said the driver, keeping his eyes on the road, his hands trembling. "Please, man. I just get paid to haul and not ask questions. If they were here you could have 'em," he said. "The buyer had them sent FedEx to his lot. Didn't want them stolen."

Chris read his eyes and believed him.

"Where's the lot?" said Chris.

"Clio. North of Flint."

No keys, no problem. Worth more intact, but these Escalades were going to be torn down for parts.

They drove down Holbrook past the massive manufacturing complex, under the giant blue overhead walkway, past the empty concrete loading docks and beyond the view of any active security cameras.

"Slow down," said Chris, near an empty field, two blocks down Holbrook. "Pull over here." The driver, who Chris guessed to be about sixty, looked as gray and pasty as the dull light reflecting on the wet street.

"No problem, man," said the driver. "Just don't shoot."

The hauler stopped with Clarence behind. He killed the Crown Vic, got out and squirted some charcoal lighter fluid out of a yellow can on the seats, dashboard and floor. He pulled a bundle of kitchen matches held together by a rubber band from the pocket of his hoodie. Clarence tossed the can of fluid into the front seat.

"You got a cell phone?" said Chris to the driver. The driver hesitated, looked down the barrel of the Glock and at Chris's no-nonsense stare.

"Yes."

"Give it up," said Chris.

The driver reached into the top pocket of his coveralls and pulled out a small, silver phone and handed it to Chris.

"Get out," said Chris. "Now."

The driver groaned as he opened the cab door and stepped down to the wet street.

"Start walking that way," said Chris, pointing to the open field. "Move it."

The driver turned and walked into the open field through the tall dead grass, shaking his head. Chris watched him trudge through the weeds and mud toward I-75. All the fields looked the same, littered with worn out tires, stained mattresses, garbage, old sofa frames with rusty coil springs exposed and plastic bags.

Clarence lit the matches and tossed them into the Crown Vic's open window. The front of the Crown Vic's interior ignited instantly. Chris heard the whump and smelled the sharp charcoal fluid vapor.

Fire engulfed the old Crown Vic. With half a tank of gas, Chris figured it would blow fast. Chris and Clarence hopped in the cab.

"I give it five minutes," said Chris. He slammed it into first and skillfully ran up through the gears.

In the side view mirror, almost six minutes later, Chris saw the Crown Vic lurch as the gas tank exploded, a large orange fireball filling the gray wet night sky.

* *

Chris pulled the hauler into a crumbling asphalt lot enclosed by a chain link fence topped with barbed wire. The fence was overgrown with vines, and the large double gate had been taken down or ripped away. The lot sat adjacent to a windowless abandoned brick and cinderblock factory. The lot held two rusty and abandoned semi-trailers.

Zippy Sanchez walked briskly from behind one of the trailers toward the hauler carrying what looked like a long, flattened screwdriver.

Chris killed the lights but kept the engine

running. Clarence jumped out of the cab before it came to a complete stop and ran to the back of the hauler. Zippy was waiting.

"Nice haul, man," he said.

"No keys," said Clarence.

A siren sounded in the distance. Clarence and Zippy stopped and turned toward the sound.

"No way," said Clarence.

"Move," said Zippy.

Chris hopped out of the cab. While Clarence dropped the loading ramp Zippy took the tool he was holding and slid it between the driver's side door frame and window on the first Escalade. With a sharp click the door lock released and Zippy hopped inside. He cracked open a cover on the steering column, gently inserted the other end of the tool, twisted it, then pressed the Escalade's ignition button. The big engine cranked then turned over. With another motion of the tool Zippy broke the steering lock. He deftly backed the Escalade off the trailer, turned the headlights off and sped out of the open gate.

The siren faded – not cop, could be an ambulance, Doppler effect indicating that it was going away from the lot, and them.

Clarence, holding a similar tool, followed suit with the next Escalade. He backed the white Escalade off the hauler, silently nodded to Chris and pulled out onto the wet, moonlit street.

Chris jacked open the door of the last Escalade when a small Suzuki security patrol vehicle pulled in the gate and stopped in front of the hauler with the brights on. Chris stopped and squinted into the light.

The door opened and a beefy, boy-faced security guard stepped out, holding a large flashlight. He stood behind the door. "Hey!" he yelled, shining the light in Chris's face. Chris pulled the Glock from his jacket pocket and walked toward the guard holding his arm straight, pointing the Glock directly at the guard's head.

"Put the light down and step away from the door," said Chris.

Laid off cop, Chris guessed. Old habits die hard. Dudes didn't make much in the first place. Long hours, every run may be their last, now they were lucky to get a little above minimum wage as security guards or mall cops. And they do shit like this?

The guard dropped the light, put his hands out to his sides and stepped away from the door.

Chris saw the fear and regret in his face. Fear for having the 9mm pointed at his forehead and regret for being stupid enough to stop where he had no business being.

"Turn around and put your hands on the trunk," said Chris.

The guard complied.

"This lot on your patrol?" said Chris.

"No," said the guard.

"Then what the fuck are you doing?" said Chris.

"Checking you out."

Chris looked at the guard, big and boyish. Common cop look. Some were ex-military types, tough and chiseled. Others were piglet looking farm boys with brush cuts.

"Ex cop, right?" asked Chris.

"Yeah."

"Where?"

"Riverview."

Chris pulled some bills from his pocket, three hundred dollars total. "Here," said Chris, putting the bills on the trunk of the car in view of the guard. "Take this. You didn't see or hear anything, right?"

The guard said nothing.

"Right?" repeated Chris. "Say it."

"Alright, alright," said the guard. "I didn't see anything."

Chris saw the guard looking at the money. "Got a family?"

"Yes."

"Take the cash and split. Buy them something nice." He pressed the Glock in the guard's back, closed in and said, "You say anything, and I'll find you and kill you. And where will that leave them? Got it?"

"Got it," said the guard.

"Early Christmas. Go." Chris motioned to the gate with the Glock. The guard picked up the roll of bills, put them in his jacket pocket and got in the little car. He backed out of the yard and drove away.

Chris pocketed the Glock, and in less than forty seconds started the Escalade and drove away, leaving the hauler empty and running in the rain.

CHAPTER 2

Elena Gets an Offer

Elena Krizi pulled the freshly washed canvass overalls from the wicker basket and attached them to the clothesline with two bottle shaped wooden pins. The sun on her tanned face felt warm and good. Elena knew this final gasp of warmth would not last much longer. The Albanian hills could turn viciously cold in a matter of hours.

Her daughter Sanja played with an old doll named Trina in the leaves and grass near Elena's bare feet.

Sanja whispered something to Trina then put the doll's head to her ear. She smiled and made the doll dance and spin.

"What's Trina doing?" said Elena.

"Dancing," said Sanja. "She wants to be a dancer." Sanja sang a little song as the doll danced. "Just like me."

Trina was Elena's doll when she was young and she felt deep satisfaction that Sanja loved it as she did. The doll was battered and worn, but still beautiful and delicate. Elena's father Milos bought the doll for her when she was six, a year older than Sanja. Milos said it looked like her. It was one of the possessions that persisted from Elena's childhood and would now be etched in Sanja's.

Sanja got up and kicked through some dry leaves. She danced with Trina, holding the doll above her head.

Elena looked at her little dancer and felt an innate urge to protect Sanja and shield her from the world. Was it possible? Maybe, with enough money and a plan. There was no money in laundry, barely enough to contribute to the family. And she was not getting any younger, even at twenty three. Elena reached and picked up another pair of overalls and two more clothespins. The wind picked up and the fresh laundry swayed in the breeze.

Milos hobbled up behind them, carrying a bucket of blueberries.

"Be careful around the clothes. Those will stain," said Elena.

"Don't worry," said Milos. He looked at Sanja. "Sanja. Come, let's wash the berries." Milos started to cough.

"Maybe you should go inside and lie down," said Elena. "Leave the berries here. I'll take care of them."

Milos, stood, trying to catch his breath.

She looked at him and patted his back. He had difficulty breathing, occasionally coughing up blood. The arthritis in his hip was eating him away. Winters were hard on him, and so was Rada, who married him after Elena's mother died, attaching herself like a tapeworm.

"Please. Go inside and lie down."

Milos smiled and nodded his head, then walked toward the cottage. She watched him slowly climb the porch.

Elena heard a motor in the distance. She cocked her head, listened, and then saw a dirty black Mercedes sedan rising on the road, gravel popping under the heavy car's tires.

Sami Neves stepped on the accelerator, his big Mercedes riding as smooth as on polished granite over the rough gravel road. He saw the small cottage through the trees and was surprised Rada was not outside waiting for him. He swung around the curve and saw Elena. She stood motionless looking at him, holding an article of clothing in her hands. What a striking young woman, even from this distance.

Elena watched the big car wind up the gravel road, her step-uncle at the wheel. "Come here," she said. She walked over to Sanja and picked her up. She looked directly at Sami, seeing his smiling face and felt uneasy and repelled, like accidentally encountering a snake.

Sami pulled in front of the square, flat roof cottage and stepped out of the Mercedes. He carried four colorful, neatly wrapped packages. Presents. He always brought presents, always Black Market.

Elena exhaled and inhaled, holding her breath and exhaling again to try and get control of her uneasiness.

She looked away from Sami. Always the same manner of dress- a gangster's uniform. Black pants, black turtleneck, black sports coat contrasting with his reddish-gray hair and beard. His dress was as dark as his eyes. Sami stared and smiled at her.

Milos stood at the front door. A wide hipped woman burst past him and rushed down the dirt walkway like a large hen. Her long braided hair swished from side to side. "Rada!" said Sami waving and smiling. Rada rushed up and hugged him.

"Sami, how wonderful to see you," she said and turned to Elena, motioning for her to come down. "Elena, hurry. Look who's here!" she said.

Elena held Sanja close to her and stood motionless, watching her step-mother and step-uncle, smiling like swamp crocodiles. So much alike, especially in the eyes, small and black. Elena walked toward them carrying Sanja and forced a smile.

"Elena," said Sami, slowly. "And little Sanja." He reached out and pinched Sanja's cheek. "You have grown so much." Sanja's face crumpled and she started to cry.

"Sanja, no need to cry," said Rada, smiling at Sami. "Look, look, Uncle Sami brought you a gift." Sanja reached out for the brightly wrapped package but Rada snatched it away. "You must wait," she said.

Sami looked straight at Elena.

"You're more beautiful every time I see you," he said.

Elena looked away and put her arms around Sanja.

"Come," said Rada. "Let's go inside."

* *

Milos sat in his worn red velour chair in front of the stone fireplace. Elena and Sanja sat on a couch and Sami sat with Rada on a floral love seat. Sami swirled raki in the small glass he held. The gifts sat at his feet.

"You still make the best," said Sami, raising the glass and sipping the white grape liquid, clear as moonshine.

"This batch turned out okay, but maybe not the best," said Milos. He doubled over, held his hand up and coughed like something was caught in his throat. After a moment Milos sat upright.

Sami sat back and looked around the damp, dark paneled room. Faded floral wallpaper, a tall wooden ledge ringing the room, festooned with plates, teacups, trinkets and black and white photographs of extended family members, some dead from the war and ancient blood feuds.

Sanja kept her eyes on the presents.

"Little Sanja," said Sami. "You would like to open your gift, no?"

Sanja smiled and nodded her head. Sami picked up Sanja's gift and handed it to her. "Here you go."

Sanja grabbed the gift and tore open the wrapping paper. Before Elena could say anything Rada said, "Sanja, what do you say to Uncle Sami?"

"Thank you," said Sanja, focusing on the wrapping paper.

Rada looked at Sami. "She gets so little."

Elena felt her temperature rise.

After ripping through the paper Sanja opened a thin white cardboard box revealing a shiny new blond doll.

"A doll," squealed Sanja. She pulled the doll from the box and hugged it.

Elena felt a rush of disappointment, hoping Sanja's instant infatuation with the doll wouldn't displace her love for Trina.

"What a beautiful dolly," said Rada.

"She could be Trina's sister," said Elena.

"Only prettier," said Rada.

Sami handed a present to Rada. She untied the bow and deftly unwrapped the colorful paper, revealing an expensive woolen cable sweater.

"For the winter," said Sami.

He handed a gift in the shape of a large coffee can to Milos. Milos thanked him and opened it.

"My favorite," said Milos, holding a can of specialty pipe tobacco.

Elena blinked. This was the very last thing that her father needed. Sami knew of Milos's health problems. His coughing.

"Now for you, Elena," said Sami. He picked up the last small package and handed it to her.

"Thank you," said Elena. She unwrapped the paper, opened a small box and took out a small jade necklace and two jade earrings.

"Oh, how beautiful," said Rada.

"Thank you very much," said Elena. They were very nice, but what would she do with them? Hang laundry in them? She held the earrings to her ears and smiled. Sami stared at her, wondering how Elena would look wearing the earrings and necklace, and nothing else.

"So how is life for you, Elena?" said Sami.

"I have no complaints."

"How are you earning your money?"

Rada put her hands on Sami's shoulder, leaning into him. "All that is available is laundry," she said. "And that is scarce."

Sami looked straight at Elena. "And what of little Sanja?" he said. "You could do much better for her."

"Anything would be an improvement," said Rada.

"Rada, please," said Elena, her face flushed. Rada glared at her with her black, pellet-like eyes. She hated it when Elena called her by her first name. She wanted Elena to call her Mother, or Nana, or any form of maternal acknowledgement. Elena settled that when she was fifteen years old, after her real mother's death.

Sami ignored Rada's comment. "I have an opportunity for you," he said to Elena.

"How exciting," said Rada.

Elena felt another flash of resentment.

"And what would that be?" said Elena.

Sami finished the raki, leaned forward and said, "One of my associates owns a very successful restaurant. In Tirana. The Blue Goose. Perhaps you have heard of it?"

Elena shook her head no.

"And?" said Rada.

I have a job for you as a server," said Sami. "You could make a lot more money. More in a month there than you would make in a year here." Sami sat back in his seat and lit a small cigar. "I had to pull many strings."

Elena pondered the novelty of having money.

"When would this happen?" she said.

"The job is waiting for you, right now," said Sami. "You can come back with me tonight."

"Tonight? That's impossible," said Elena, stunned.

"Yes, tonight," said Sami.

"What about Sanja?" said Elena.

"Sanja will stay here with us," said Rada.

Elena looked around the room, speechless. She felt the impulse to rush and take Sanja from here as far and fast as she could. Milos stood and softly said, "It's a good opportunity for you. You can bring in money, for your future. And Sanja's."

Elena stared dumbfounded at Milos. "You knew about this?" she said.

"How can we go on like this?" Rada screeched. "Papa and I will not last forever. What is your future here? Laundry the rest of your life? We can barely support ourselves, let alone you and Sanja."

Sami intensified. "You will make good money

to send home. For Sanja. To build a life for yourself."

Elena felt ambushed and defeated. Where would she go if she did grab Sanja and run? In the woods? Out in the fields, facing the land mines that were everywhere, left over from the war?

"I will have to think," she said.

"It is decided," said Rada.

Elena sprang to her feet. "You decide my life?"

Milos raised his hand and said, "Elena, I hate it as much as you but it is the only way."

"And what are your prospects here?" said Rada. "Who will have you?"

Elena rushed from the room.

CHAPTER 3

Chop Shop

Chris was the last one to pull into the big yard. A small white and red sign on the barbed wire chain link fence read ACE Salvage. If there was a market for bootleg barbed wire, Chris thought, Detroit was a gold mine. Zippy manned the gate and Chris drove through with the lights off and stopped. Zippy closed the sliding gate, locked it with a padlock then got in the front seat of the black Escalade alongside Chris.

"Nice ride, man," he said. "Bling machine."

"Not bad," said Chris. "I'm not much of a bling guy."

"No bling, no personality, no pussy," said Zippy. "You got to get you some. All three."

They drove past derelict car bodies, some totaled, looking almost new in the rear but with entire front ends torn apart or missing. The windshields had opaque spider web cracks where the unlucky passengers slammed their heads.

Chris spotted two cars that had been wrapped around trees. Good for some parts, but there were always scraps of hair, skin, blood and bone fragments in the interiors. Always.

They pulled in front of the gray corrugated steel building and before hopping out Zippy said, "Know what you need? Big booty Hispanic ho. Do you like nobody else. I'll hook you up."

Zippy laughed and walked to the large metal door and pressed the green UP button on the side. The chain drive contactor snapped and the door rumbled upward. As soon as it cleared the roof of the Escalade Chris pulled in.

* *

Chris got tight with Zippy back in Juvie, winding up there via an incident skipping school with one of his friends. Chris was done with school and wanted to drop out, but Michigan law required parental permission and no one knew where his father was.

Chris was at his buddy's house, smoking weed and watching porn on VHS. His buddy's recently divorced mother went away with a new guy for the weekend. Getting the munchies from the weed, they took his mother's big Chrysler Imperial and drove to the corner party store. Chris rode shotgun. His buddy was wasted and instead of hitting the brakes, stomped on the accelerator and drove through the party store's front window. Panicked, Chris grabbed the steering wheel and rammed into a man at the counter buying lottery tickets, nearly killing him. They were busted and Chris was sentenced to three years in the Wayne County Juvenile Detention Facility, on Monroe Street near Greektown.

Zippy was busted for the third time when he was fourteen years old for breaking into cars and stealing in-dash stereos. He worked for his brother Jesus, who was boosting cars Grand Theft Auto style for years. Did time for it once. The cops tried to intimidate Zippy into giving up Jesus, but Zippy kept his mouth shut and was given five years.

Chris and Zippy became pals in auto shop class. Chris liked Zippy's quick wit and sense of humor. Chris was smart and cool headed and Zippy discovered Chris was naturally good with cars. They worked on every old beater that showed up in class. A lot of car knowledge absorbed by Zippy via Jesus rubbed off on Chris. After two years they could fix, or hack into, anything on wheels. That's what they considered themselves- hackers. Just like the computer geeks, only Chris and Zippy did it with iron, glass, wires, rubber and sheet metal.

* *

The first Escalade was already well into being stripped, on cinder blocks, doors and fenders off, engine on a hoist like an excised heart. Jesus and Clarence were busy with saws and impact wrenches working the Escalades over. Zippy picked up a pneumatic impact wrench, revved it a couple of times and started taking the front seat out of the second Escalade.

Chris parked behind the other vehicles, all in a row, just like an assembly line. Funny thing about cars. Expensive enough in the first place but ten times the cost if the parts were bought individually. Engine, tranny, differential, wheels, fresh brake rotors, radiators, catalytic converters, whatever, were worth a fortune on the underground market. Even some of the legit auto parts stores dealt in these, marked as remanufactured.

Eddie Siegler sat in his motorized wheelchair, supervising. Next to him stood a large, powerful looking man in a black track suit with a thin white stripe running down the jacket and pants. Foreign, was Chris's first thought. Even the Mafia guys didn't dress like that anymore. Eddie waved for Chris to come over. Chris got out of the Escalade, took off his driving gloves and walked toward them.

"What took you so long?" asked Eddie.

"Security guard. Ex cop," said Chris. "No big deal. Cost three hundred bucks, though. You got it covered?"

"No problem," said Eddie. He looked at the man in the track suit. "This is a new friend of ours. Name's Vlad." Eddie briefly pointed to the Escalades. "This is his order."

"Good price for parts," said Vlad in a thick accent.

"Yes there is," said Chris.

Vlad eyeballed Chris. "More value, though, in Mercedes and BMW," he said. "Even though I drive Cadillac."

Typical European, thought Chris. Everything was better over there. No matter what it was. If everything was better there then what was he doing here?

Eddie laughed, gave Chris a look, then said to Vlad, "Mercedes. BMWs. We can do those. No problem."

This Vlad guy was big. Big and in good shape, looked like in his fifties. A lot of guys that age were powerhouses. This dude was different from what Chris had seen of the Eastern European gangster types. Clean cut. Most of them were big and heavy, wearing dense leather coats, had greasy long hair, some with beards. This dude was clean shaven and had a buzz cut.

Chris knew Eddie was hooked up with the Italians, deep, but not with this guy.

Eddie had a few sweet deals going and he spread them out. One was the key-cutting operation at a few dealerships. He had a couple of guys on the inside that cut keys using VINs of new cars on the lot. An order comes in, get the keys, unlock the cars, and drive away. Easy as shit. Then, go buy some used models similar to the stolen cars and retag the stolen cars with the clean VINs. Cops would run them down if someone got pulled over, and they'd come up legit. Eddie sold the cars to the Italians for cheap, but still made a good profit. The Italians sold them all over New Jersey and New York. Eddie made sure the rosette rivets for the VIN plates were well accounted for and well hidden, since possession of rosette rivets was a four-year felony.

Eddie liked doing things the easy way. Grab the low hanging fruit, take on the more difficult specialized jobs later, like the Escalade boost that Chris engineered. A car parked anywhere was a low-hanger and fair game. Just tow 'em away. That's how Clarence got hooked up with ACE Salvage, working with one of his mother's many boyfriends. One of them drove a freelance tow truck and just picked up cars off the street. The tow truck driver also did a lot of repos, carried a 38 and sometimes dealt with irate, violent deadbeats. Having Clarence along was a benefit. Clarence was short, but had muscles and knew how to fight, street style.

The tow truck driver broke Clarence in, teaching him how to prep cars for towing, how to bust ignition locks, how to jack them right off the street and how to instantly pop open a locked door through the top of a rolled up window. Clarence caught on fast.

Chris didn't notice Clarence glaring at him for not diving in to do the hard, gut-busting work of tearing down the Escalades. Clarence turned and pumped the handle of a leaky hydraulic jack, raising the rear end of an Escalade.

Eddie handed Chris an envelope containing seventy five hundred dollars cash. The Escalades ran around seventy two thousand new, off lease around fifty five or sixty, which put the total around one hundred and eighty thousand. His take was around four percent, which wasn't bad. More to stash for the TradeWind.

"What about the three hundred?" said Chris.

Vlad took out his wallet and pulled out three bills from a stack of hundreds and handed them to Chris.

Chris put the bills in the envelope, opened his jacket, revealing the handle of the Glock. He put the envelope in an interior pocket.

"Glock nine millimeter," said Vlad.

"Works every time," said Chris.

Vlad looked at Chris, coolly. "This has worked out very well. Very efficient," he said. "Eddie tells me you organize and execute these, how you say, boosts?"

"I do my best."

"Maybe you could do some work for me sometime," said Vlad.

Chris smiled. He wondered why Eddie would take on orders from this dude, with all he had already going on. The big guy towered over Eddie like a hawk over a field mouse. Eddie looked frail in his wheelchair compared to this giant. Maybe Eddie's body was broken, but not his brain, so Chris figured he was up to something that would bring in a lot of fresh cash.

"Speaking of work," said Chris, looking at the crew stripping the Escalades. He nodded and walked over to Zippy. Zippy had the two front seats unbolted from the Escalade and Chris helped him pull them out.

Zippy yelled out to Clarence, "Hey asshole. Get to work!"

Clarence looked at Zippy.

Zippy made a face and laughed.

Clarence turned back into his work, removing the brake rotor from the left rear axle.

"C'mon, man," said Chris. "Don't piss off Clarence. Seriously. He's moody today. He liked that Crown Vic."

Chris saw Vlad bend down and say something to Eddie. Eddie nodded. The big guy turned and walked out.

Two hours later the Escalade parts were stripped and boxed, most of the parts oiled and wrapped in waxy paper. Eddie was hidden in his office. Chris washed up in a dirty sink with a green bar of Lava then walked to the office.

Eddie sat behind his Cold War vintage gray metal desk.

"What's up with the Russian?" said Chris.

"Albanian," said Eddie.

"Whatever," said Chris. "What's this guy all about, anyway? Don't you have enough going on? And what about the Italians? They don't like competition."

Eddie smiled at Chris's brashness. "Do I tell you how to steal cars? No." He wheeled around from behind the desk. "Don't tell me how to run my operation."

"These dudes are nasty from what I hear, man. Russians, Albanians," said Chris. He looked down at Eddie in the chair. "The Italians at least let everyone know what the rules are, and they stick to them. They got a system and so do we. And it works. What do you know about this guy? How can you trust him?" Chris crouched down a little and looked right into Eddie's eyes. "And what's this shit about me working for him?"

"Don't worry about it," said Eddie. "I got it covered. Vlad's up and coming, and connected downtown," he said. "He's big time in Eastern Europe, Canada too. Protected. He's got plans. Big ones."

"I still don't like it," said Chris.

Eddie wheeled back to his desk and looked down at some papers.

"You don't have to," he said without looking up.

* *

Chris walked out through the back of the garage. He put on his black helmet, fired up his Fat Boy, feeling the low Harley rumble and rolled out of the junkyard. Stealing cars was a calculated risk. Conducting a criminal enterprise- twenty years, a hundred thousand dollars plus forfeiture of everything related. Operating a chop shop- ten years, two hundred and fifty thousand dollars plus mandatory restitution. Intent to pass false title- ten years and five thousand dollars. Receiving and concealing a motor vehicle- five years and ten thousand dollars.

Grand theft auto- three years usually, and three

years probation after that, even for a first offense. Since Chris helped strip the cars he could also be charged with operating and concealing. They all had a lot to lose. Eddie better know what he was doing...

Chris gunned the Harley, got on Woodward and headed south toward Jefferson. He planned on throwing the keys to the torched Crown Vic and the driver's cell phone into the Detroit River.

CHAPTER 4

Elena Gets Duped

Sami drove fast through the narrow mountain road for hours then connected on SH2 toward Tirana. The night was still and warm and the bright moon cast silver light on the trees. Elena stared out the window, rolling the situation over and over in her mind. Being separated from Sanja was killing her, even in these short hours on the road. She worried about Sanja being alone with Rada. What if Sanja did something to make Rada angry and Milos wasn't home?

There was logic in her leaving. Making money, getting her own place, sending for Sanja. Putting her in school, maybe Sanja could be somebody. Who knows, Elena thought, I could maybe meet someone…. It might not be so bad after all. Elena took off her shoes, reclined in the seat and fell asleep.

Sami slowed the big Mercedes and pulled off SH2 near Rruga Marqinet on the distant outskirts of Tirana. He drove a few kilometers as Elena

27

slept, crossed railroad tracks slowly as not to wake her, then stopped in front of a small, two story corrugated metal warehouse with blackened windows. Sami quietly stepped out of the car and walked toward the building and rapped on the large steel door. He heard techno music through the thick door, thumping and continuous. He saw a shadow cross the peephole and the door opened.

A thick bouncer looked Sami up and down. Jerzy Vogodian stood at the bouncer's side. "Well, well," he said. "My old friend. What have you brought me?"

"Come see," said Sami. "Her name is Elena."

Jerzy nodded to the bouncer and followed Sami outside. They walked to the Mercedes where Elena still slept. Sami opened the passenger door and said, "Elena. Wake up. Step outside." Elena opened her eyes and momentarily was not sure where she was. She blinked, looked at the building then at Sami, standing and smiling with another man at his side.

"We will stop here awhile," said Sami. "Let's get something to eat and drink."

Elena, confused, looked at Jerzy. "Hello, Elena," he said.

"This is Jerzy, an old friend of mine," said Sami. "Come," he said, motioning for Elena to get out of the car. "Let's go inside." Elena, still cloudy from sleep, put on her shoes and stepped out of the car, momentarily revealing her long, tanned legs through her loose cotton dress. Jerzy looked at Sami and said "Very nice. You were telling the truth."

"What was that?" said Elena.

"Nothing," said Sami. "Let's go inside."

They walked through the door and entered the

building, techno music pounding. Elena's eyes adjusted to the dim light. Blue cigarette smoke hung in the room. A large mirrored disco ball suspended from the ceiling rotated and reflected red and blue light. The shards of light bounced off the foil covered walls. The floor was strewn with velour sofas, love seats and chairs. A sign above the long, lacquered black bar read in English MANHATTAN DISCO.

A girl danced topless in a g-string on a dark stage, swinging on a pole and grooving to the beat. Men laughed and hung around the stage, grabbing at her. Other girls danced topless around the stage. One nude girl swooned in a man's lap on one of the big velour chairs.

Elena stopped, shocked, mouth open. A naked woman brushed against her carrying a tray with a bottle of champagne and two flutes. The woman smelled of Chanel, sweat and sex.

"What kind of place is this?" asked Elena. She felt sick and out of place. Violated. Why would Sami bring her here?

Jerzy laughed "A very good one, my sweet." Sami laughed also. "This is not the way I remembered it," he said to Elena.

"Come, follow me," said Jerzy. They passed by the dancing girls and the bar. The naked woman on the man's lap now stood holding the man's hand, leading him toward a staircase. Sami, Elena and Jerzy passed through a small archway to a back room, furnished with three old dining tables.

"Please," said Jerzy, holding Elena's chair. "Sit." Elena sat and Jerzy, acting as the perfect gentleman, pushed in her chair. "What would you like to drink?" he asked. "We have some very fine champagne."

"Vodka for me," said Sami. "Elena?"

Elena said "Just Coke, please."

"Nothing stronger?" said Jerzy.

"No," said Elena. "Coke is fine. Thank you."

Jerzy smiled widely at Sami, revealing his brown, tobacco stained teeth. "Very polite," he said. "I like that." He got up from the table and walked through the archway to the bar.

Elena turned to Sami. "I would like to go, please."

"No, no," said Sami, lighting a thin cigar. "It would be rude. We will leave shortly, but let us show Jerzy a little courtesy. Just one drink, and a little food." Sami leaned back in his chair and exhaled a burst of blue smoke. "Besides, I would like to rest for awhile. It's a long drive, and after all, I'm doing this for you." Elena heard a woman laughing hysterically over the music in the room by the bar.

"Alright," said Elena. "But one drink, please. I would still like to leave."

At the bar, Jerzy poured four shot glasses full of vodka and filled a small glass with ice and Coke. He pulled two pills from a small tin box he carried and dropped them into the Coke. He waited until they dissolved. He put the shots and the Coke on a small tray, put a serving towel over his forearm and returned to the table.

Jerzy smiled at Sami and Elena. "You should take a picture," he said. "It's very unusual I do this, like a waiter." He placed the Coke in front of Elena and two shot glasses in front of Sami and two where he was sitting. He put the tray in the middle of the table, sat down and raised a shot glass.

"To friends!" he said.

Elena half smiled and lifted her glass. Sami and Jerzy looked at each other and downed the shots.

Elena sipped the Coke.

"Drink up, Elena," said Sami. "Are you sure you don't want anything stronger? To relax you?"

"No, this is fine," said Elena.

Jerzy laughed and raised the other glass. "How they say, down the hatch?" He drained the shot glass as did Sami. Elena took another sip of Coke and swallowed.

"Please excuse me," she said. "I need to use the toilet. Please, can you tell me where it is?"

"I'm so sorry," said Jerzy. "I am a bad host, I will show you. It is by the stairway."

Elena stood up and wobbled, feeling dizzy, like the blood was draining from her head. Her legs felt unstable and heavy. She steadied herself on her chair. The relentless pounding of the techno sounded distant and abstract.

"Are you alright, my dear?" said Sami.

Feeling a bit more steady, Elena, said "Yes, just very tired from the drive, I suppose." She walked with Jerzy to the stairway, then stood still and held her head in her hands. The room spun, and her knees buckled. Jerzy steadied her, then held her as Elena broke into a cold sweat. "Wha...?" she said then the room went black.

Jerzy held her limp body in his arms and carried her up the stairway. Light as a feather, he thought, but enough flesh in the right places. He kicked a half open door and laid her on an unkempt bed. Jerzy made sure she was secure underneath a quilt, walked out of the room and locked the door. He went down the stairs and sat at the table with Sami.

"She is as beautiful as you said. Very fresh," said Jerzy.

"I told you," said Sami. "When have I lied to you?"

"Let me count the times," said Jerzy.

Sami laughed. "I'll be on my way," he said. "Let's settle."

Jerzy sat back in his chair. "Ten thousand is a lot of money."

"But we agreed," said Sami.

Jerzy's face turned to stone. "Yes we agreed." He pulled an envelope stuffed with bills from his green sports jacket pocket. "Five thousand. American dollars. Times are difficult. It's a fair price."

Sami's face twisted and turned red. "For diseased dogs, maybe. We agreed to ten thousand. Deutschmarks."

Jerzy smiled. "Diseased dogs," he said. "That's good. We save those for the NATO soldiers."

Sami snatched the envelope, opened it and started counting.

"It's all there," said Jerzy.

"Like I can trust you," said Sami, counting the bills.

"That is more than generous," said Jerzy.

Sami put the envelope back on the table. "Maybe we will forget the entire deal."

Jerzy leaned forward and looked directly into Sami's eyes. "Sami, my old friend. Do not try to do that."

"Friend?" said Sami. He shook his head and looked at the envelope.

Jerzy pointed to it. "Take the money and leave, before you say or do something foolish." Sami gazed at the stairway for a moment, then picked up the envelope and put it in his jacket pocket.

"This is the last of us," he said.

"That makes me sad," said Jerzy. "But business is business. This is the system."

Sami stood, turned and walked toward the

entrance. Jerzy followed, glancing at the bouncer.

"Are you sure you would not like to stay awhile?" said Jerzy. "Give me a chance to earn back the money I gave you?" Jerzy motioned to two girls standing near the bar. Sami said nothing, walked past the bouncer, got in the Mercedes and drove away into the night.

CHAPTER 5

Bait Car Blues

After tossing the Crown Vic keys and cell phone into the Detroit River, Chris took Jefferson back to Woodward, turned right, maneuvered the Harley through the traffic circle around Campus Martius and cruised past the plain white work van parked near the Fox Theatre.

Investigator Freeman Washington sat in the van's shotgun seat, Big Bill Purdy in the driver's and Walter Robbins in the rear. Robbins manned the radio, kill box and laptop.

"Ping it once more," said Washington, looking across the street at a burgundy Chevy Avalanche. Robbins positioned the cursor to an icon on the laptop display and clicked the mouse. The small vehicle icon turned yellow momentarily, then turned green.

"Good to go," said Robbins.

Washington watched the Avalanche. Great bait car, parts in demand, especially around Southwest border towns, being a vehicle of choice for some of the bigger Mexican drug gangs. Sometimes they let vehicles walk, just like guns, ATF style. Mark the parts and see where they show up, occasionally leading to a bigger bust. But that was ATF and not the Detroit Police Department, Auto Theft Unit. Washington didn't like to see anything walk.

"Man I'm hungry," said Purdy.

"You're always hungry," said Washington.

"Old lady's on this diet kick. No more chili fries. No more conies. No more Lafayette. Now, it's mostly turkey, chicken and lettuce. I hate that shit," said Purdy.

"So?" said Robbins. "Stop by American. You won't be lying if she asks if you went to Lafayette."

"She'll know," said Purdy. "She's got spies everywhere," he said, looking at Washington.

Washington looked at his watch. 1:30AM. If nothing happened in another four hours, the bait car would be moved and his shift would be done. The hours and the shifts were getting tough. He was beginning to feel weary, feel his age. Twenty two years, winding up working midnights. That's the way it worked here. Something happens years ago and you're labeled for life. Just like that. Like a regular actor doing porn- only has to do it one time and the career is shot. Once the brass thinks you're trigger happy, that's it. Lawyers loved it. Get shot by a cop who's quick to pull the trigger and it's a big time payday.

The stakeouts were long and mostly boring, like fishing, but with the same allure. Sometimes a fish would hit the bait, sometimes not. Just had to be in the right water at the right time, and this was the right water. The right time was just a matter of luck. Washington thought about the muskie starting to hit, moving down from Lake St. Claire, through the Detroit River to Lake Erie. The water was cooling off and the fish were cold, hungry, big and firm, going after smaller bait fish. He looked forward to going fishing after his shift. Grab his tackle box, pole, face the cold and head down to the RiverWalk.

A short dude in a black hoodie turned the corner and stopped in front of the Avalanche. He looked around and jacked open the door. The car alarm sounded. Didn't matter. There wasn't a soul that paid any attention to those.

Washington straightened in his seat.

"Fish on," he said. "Call one-ten."

Robbins got on the radio. "One-ten. Five-o-three. Repeat, five-o-three, over."

No reply.

The Avalanche took off going west on Montcalm toward Woodward Avenue.

"Fish is running," said Washington. "Move."

Purdy slammed the van into drive and jammed down the accelerator. Robbins flew out of his seat and Washington felt the gees push him back. Robbins scrambled and toggled the button on the radio. "One-ten. Five-o-three. Repeat, five-o-three. You copy?"

Dead air. "Nobody there," said Robbins.

"Shit," said Washington. "Kill it."

The Avalanche shot through the red light, zoomed across Woodward past Comerica Park and headed toward Brush Street. Robbins, back in his seat, flipped a red toggle switch on a small electrical box mounted on the surface of a bench with the Velcroed laptop. This sent a signal to a receiver hidden in the Avalanche. The signal shut off the flow of gasoline to the big engine's fuel injectors. The vehicle slowed, no matter how hard the Fish pumped the accelerator. The Avalanche rolled to a complete stop at the corner of Montcalm and Brush.

Washington pulled his service revolver as the van approached the stalled Avalanche. The Fish jumped from the cabin and ran. Fast. Purdy squealed the van to a stop.

"C'mon," said Washington. He opened the door and yelled, "Halt. Police!"

Almost ballet-like the Fish pulled a semiautomatic pistol from his pocket and fired toward Washington and the van. Sounded like popcorn. One bullet whizzed by Washington's head and shattered the window on the open van door. The other shots went *ping ping ping* into the door body. Washington hit the ground, took aim and fired a round, just missing the Fish's head.

The Fish ran sideways and fired another wild burst of gunfire then sprinted around the corner down Brush. Washington ran, but stopped when he saw the young, agile Fish race across Brush along the front of Ford Field.

Purdy caught up to Washington, put his hands on his knees and head down, winded. "I'm too flippin' fat for this," he said, trying to catch his breath. Washington gazed down Brush, the Fish now long gone. Where was the goddamn blue and white?

CHAPTER 6

The Bunker

The Bunker, as the DPD precinct station was called, sat between the massive green glass towers of the Renaissance Center and Hart Plaza, a surreal space with a circular metal sculpture like a portal to another dimension and an overhead fountain and floor that resembled an industrial washbasin. Slung low, made of rough concrete and dark glass with angled walls, the Bunker faced the Detroit River like a pillbox on the beaches of Normandy.

Washington sat in the small debriefing area. Inspector Andre Davenport walked in with a blond, neatly dressed woman. A Fed, thought Washington. He could spot them a galaxy away. So now what, some Fed telling him what to do? Every Fed he encountered in his twenty two years on the job carried this air of superiority and arrogance. Every single one.

"All right," said Davenport. "I've read your report." Davenport gestured to the woman. "This is agent Ann Peabody. DEA." Peabody nodded.

Washington nodded then acted like she wasn't there.

"Where was our backup?" asked Washington.

"The log says one-ten along with two other units was dispatched to a triple homicide. On Fernhill, off of Woodward. Near Seven Mile. Place was boarded up. Found a girl chained to a toilet. Fourteen years old, been missing two weeks. Shot dead, along with two men. Looks like both wanted her for themselves, one shot the girl out of spite, then they shot each other."

"We should have been notified," said Washington.

"Dispatch should have contacted you. I can't argue with that, but it is what it is," said Davenport. "These things happen."

Over the years Washington learned the art of letting things go. Got good at identifying battles that couldn't be won. This was one of them. Washington looked at Peabody. "DEA and auto? I don't get it," he said.

"Agent Peabody can use our help," said Davenport.

"Hello Investigator Washington," she said, holding out her hand. Washington reluctantly shook it. "I'm Ann Peabody, Special Agent, DEA. I'm in Detroit for a reason," she said.

Washington nodded. The woman was compact, thin but muscular. Her handshake was strong and cool to the touch.

"I'll get right to the point," said Peabody. We believe a new heroin distribution route may be established here in Detroit, but we have no direct evidence," she said. "We believe there's an Albanian connection. We're looking at one individual in particular."

She opened the case to a tablet computer, turned it on and within a couple of swipes a photograph appeared on the bright screen. A photograph of Vlad Dragovic.

"This is a person of interest," said Peabody. "His name is Vlad Dragovic. They call him 'The Dragon'. We believe he's well connected in Albania and perhaps Turkey. He's a legal resident here in Detroit. Along with heroin, we believe he's involved in auto theft, human trafficking, kidnapping, prostitution, illegal gambling, to name a few."

Peabody studied Washington's face. "We know he owns a few legitimate businesses, several laundromats, interest in some restaurants, real estate," she said. "Pretty mundane stuff. He also owns a strip club on Eight Mile Road, called the Tiger's Den. We would take him down there but he's operating within the law and we can't get anyone inside."

Washington looked at the photo of Vlad. Big guy. Muscular, lean, especially for his age. Definitely take some firepower to put this dude down.

"We haven't had any luck infiltrating Albanian gangs," said Peabody. "Used to be the Italians ran things, drugs, gambling, prostitution, along with the Russians. Not so much anymore."

Peabody twirled a silver pen. "The Albanians are incredibly tough," she said. "Ruthless. Pure old country, not like the Italians or Greeks who've been here a few generations. Everything is done with a handshake. Called the Besa," said Peabody. "They live and die by the Besa."

"We're seeing some Albanian activity in these parts, but they seem to be a blip on the radar," said Davenport.

"That's because they have a relatively low profile and keep quiet, no matter what," said Peabody. "Think the Italians have a code of silence?"

Washington nodded. Godfather stuff. "Omerta," he said.

"Right," said Peabody. "But occasionally someone in the mob will flip and go into witness or prisoner protection. Look what happened in New York a few years ago. One guy flips and takes down the top bosses, walks clean and moves into witness protection."

Peabody tapped the pen against her index finger. "Not these people. Albanians don't flip. Period. They live and die by the Kanun," she said. "Means code. Goes all the way back to the fifteenth century."

"What is that?" asked Washington.

"It's a code of honor," said Peabody. "There where Besa comes into play. Break a Besa and it usually results in a blood feud between clans."

Peabody looked squarely at Davenport and Washington.

"People die," she said. "Sometimes a lot of them. It's called 'being in the blood'. It's all about honor and revenge. After the initial murder, the other side kills someone in the opposing clan, and if it's not the original offender, then any male will do," said Peabody. "In rare cases, females. It goes back and forth."

"Like the Bloods and the Crips," said Davenport.

"Only more intense," said Peabody. She picked up the tablet computer and swiped, showing a map of Albania, Turkey and Italy. "Especially since drugs came into the picture." Peabody enlarged the map around Milan, Italy. "In the early days the Albanians partnered with the Italians, then struck off on their own. A lot still happens in and around Milan," she said, looking down at the map. "Milan is an intersection of sorts for gangs from Kosovo, supporting the KLA," she said.

"The KLA?" asked Washington.

"Kosovo Liberation Army," said Peabody. "The gangs in Milan help supply what's left of the KLA with weapons." Peabody swiped the map and enlarged the image of Albania.

"Heroin comes in through what's called the Balkan Route. Starts in Turkey, goes through Greece, Bulgaria, Albania, the Czech Republic, Hungary, Austria, Germany and Italy," said Peabody. She stood with her hands on her hips. "Heroin flows in, up to fifty kilos a day."

"Fifty keys..." said Davenport. He put his hand to his chin, mentally calculating.

"That's around one hundred and ten pounds," said Peabody, "which has a street value of around eight million, eight hundred thousand dollars." She picked up the tablet. "A day. Not counting the cocaine."

Peabody flipped back to the photo of Vlad.

"Make no mistake," she said. "We're dealing with one of the most powerful drug organizations in the world."

"Didn't really know that much about them, to tell the truth," said Washington.

"I'm not surprised," said Peabody. "They live very, very humbly. Only a few of the top bosses live large. Their code of silence and revenge play into it big time," she said. "Wrong somebody, talk, it not only comes back to you, but your entire family."

She looked squarely at Washington and Davenport.

"It's more than just money to some of them," she said. "It's a cause. A lot of the cash still goes to the KLA." She looked down at the photo of Vlad. "This guy is different. We think he might go rogue. We think he's got ambition and is going outside the clans."

Peabody looked at Washington.

"That's where you can help us," she said. "We also think he's involved in an auto theft ring, here in Detroit." She turned off the tablet computer and closed the leather case. "That might be the best and easiest path to get to this guy and to the heroin. That and the strip club." She looked at Washington. "Inspector Davenport says you're cool under fire. And, we're aware of your record."

Washington straightened.

"Whoa," he said. "Who are you to talk about my record? I don't know you, and you certainly don't know me," said Washington, staring Peabody directly in the eye, then shifting to Davenport.

"What Agent Peabody is saying is that you're a resource. A valuable one," said Davenport.

Peabody piped in. "A major part of your job is surveillance," she said. "And you're good at it. Patient and effective, according to Inspector Davenport. I respect that," she said. "And frankly, you're not afraid to act."

"Agent Peabody can use you to help watch this guy," said Davenport, pointing to the rendering of Vlad.

"What about auto?" said Washington. "That's my thing. Always has been."

"This is auto for the most part," said Davenport. "At least for ninety days. This goes all the way up to the Chief."

"What about Purdy and Robbins?" asked Washington.

"They'll be there when you need them." Davenport leaned forward. "Look," he said. "Other units are being cut or scaled back, more and more going over to gangs, homicide. That's just how we have to roll," he said. "You know the system."

"The system," said Washington.

CHAPTER 7

Elena Wakes

Elena opened her unfocused eyes, the room painfully bright. Her head pounded with every beat of her heart. She pushed off the quilt and sat up, causing the dull pain in her head to sharpen. The bed smelled sour and the sheets were stained, as if they hadn't been changed in weeks. The taste in her mouth was metallic and her throat was dry, making it difficult to swallow.

A woman sat across the room at a cheap white vanity, looking in a mirror. The woman, Miri, showing signs of age put filler in the wrinkles around her mouth and eyes.

Elena looked at Miri, watching her work meticulously on her face, wearing nothing but a thin, transparent pink robe. Elena noticed Miri's little finger on her left hand was missing.

"Where am I?" said Elena. "Where is Sami?"

"Who is Sami?" said Miri, dryly, not turning from the mirror.

"My step uncle. We were going to Tirana."

"Tirana," said Miri. "That might as well be on the moon."

"Please, I must go," said Elena. "There is some mistake," she said, blinded by the shooting pain in her head.

"You cannot go," said Miri. "Jerzy owns you now. You belong to him, as I do. All of us here do."

"What?" said Elena.

"Take my advice and accept it," said Miri. She smiled. "You are very beautiful. And young. You should do well. At least for a while." Miri dabbed her cheek with a makeup brush. "I wonder how much Jerzy paid for you?"

"Paid for me?" said Elena.

The bedroom door lock clicked, the door opened and Jerzy walked in. Miri quickly turned back to the vanity and her makeup.

"I see you are awake," said Jerzy.

"Where is Sami?" said Elena.

"He is gone," said Jerzy. His expression turned cold. "Now stand up."

"Why?" said Elena.

Jerzy slapped Elena across her face, her head snapping to one side.

"Stand up."

Elena, shocked and reeling from the slap started to cry. She stood.

"Why are you doing this?" she said.

Jerzy fondled her auburn hair. "Such beautiful hair. Soft." He put his hand up her dress on her crotch.

Anger rose deep within Elena, white hot, overriding the sharp pain in her head. She hit Jerzy with both fists, pounding at him. Jerzy punched her in the ribs, knocking her back on the bed. Elena couldn't breath, as much as she wanted and tried to, having the wind knocked out of her. She stared at the ceiling. After a moment she drew in a deep, uncontrolled breath, her ribs and side feeling empty and on fire.

"Bring me the kit," said Jerzy.

Miri quickly opened a drawer of the vanity and pulled out a black pouch containing a hypodermic needle and teaspoon and took it to Jerzy.

"Light a candle."

Miri took a match from a small book of matches and lit a candle on the nightstand next to the bed. Jerzy pulled out a small, sugar-sized brown paper packet of heroin, put it in the teaspoon and held it over the candle. The heroin melted and he filled the hypodermic.

"Hold her."

Miri went to the bed and straddled Elena and held her down. Elena, reeling from the punch, spacey and detached looked up at Miri. Jerzy took Elena's right arm and tapped the soft inside flesh with two fingers, raising a vein. He injected the heroin into Elena's arm.

Within a few seconds Elena felt sick to her stomach, then came a wild rush of pleasure and relief. She felt as if she floated, soft and airy as a cloud. Then she lost consciousness.

* *

Elena vaguely felt something heavy and someone in her. She lay on her back, her legs spread and tied to two lower wooden bedposts. Her arms were tied to two top posts by strips of a torn cotton sheet. She drifted into consciousness with a man sweating on top of her, his garlic and vodka laced breath washing over her like a blanket of putrid fog. He let out a succession of thrusts and grunts, pulled out, stood and put his pants on. He turned and strolled out of the bedroom.

Elena tugged at the bindings. Her eyes felt on fire and the smell, her own and that of the man made her stomach churn. She vaguely remembered Jerzy coming into the room and putting the needle in her arm. How many times? Two? Three? It sent her back to the cloud of warmth and calm. Now she was cold, hungry and had to pee. Bad.

The door opened and Miri walked in, carrying a bottle of water. She sat on the bed next to Elena. Elena looked up at her, her mouth too dry to talk. Miri untied her arms and legs and helped her sit upright, trying to ignore the smell. The smell and Elena's eyes. She saw it before and it was the same every time, Jerzy creating another addict. Just get them dependent enough, but not ruin their looks.

"Here, drink this," said Miri, twisting the cap off the bottle of water. She held it to Elena's mouth. Elena took the bottle and drank, her wrists red and chaffed from the tight strips of sheet. After downing the bottle of water, she whispered, "toilet."

"Come," said Miri. "I'll take you. You can take a shower. I will get you something to eat." Miri helped Elena to her feet. Elena's legs felt elastic and unsteady and her crotch was sore and burning.

"I'm to help you," said Miri. "Jerzy told me to. If you obey and do what you need to do, life may not be so bad. If you don't..."

Elena used the toilet and showered, feeling the hot water run down her face and body like liquid sunshine. She slowly washed her hair and felt the pain in her head dissipate. She was relieved to have the man's sweat and stink off of her. Elena toweled off slowly, then felt incredibly hungry.

"I need something to eat," said Elena. Miri handed her a robe and lead her back to the bedroom.

"Stay here," said Miri. "I'll bring you back something."

Elena stood in front of the vanity for a moment then sat, letting out a squeal of pain. It hurt to sit. She put her head in her hands, arm propped up by her elbows. The temporary relief of the shower was wearing off. She felt cold and her skin began to itch. No– *crawl*.

Miri walked in the bedroom carrying clean sheets. Balanced on the sheets was a plate holding a bowl of soup and a small loaf of brown bread.

"Here, eat this," said Miri. Elena stood and took the plate holding the bowl of soup and bread, put it on the vanity and started eating. Miri stripped the dank, sweat and semen soaked sheets from the bed and tossed them in a pile on the wooden floor.

"You must do what Jerzy tells you to do. Everything. You need to do what you have to do to survive," said Miri.

Elena swallowed a hunk of bread, looked at the bed and said, "How long was I tied there?"

"Two days," said Miri. "Two days and at least fifteen men. Very light duty."

It was all fog to Elena. She remembered the needle, some men, sometimes feeling good, and the highs.

"Do as he says, and it will not be so bad for you," said Miri. "Do as he says and he will not shoot you up so much. Trust me," she said. "It will ruin you."

Elena felt a tremor from seeing the needle

pierce and sting her arm, but liked the calm and happiness shortly after. The pleasant detachment…and wanted it again. She wrapped her arms around herself, hunched over and rocked.

The door opened. Jerzy walked in and stood over Elena. Elena looked up at him.

"Please," she said softly. "Where is Sami? I'm not supposed to be here."

"That's were you're wrong," said Jerzy. "This is exactly where you're supposed to be."

"But Sami," said Elena.

"Enough Sami," said Jerzy. "You're mine now. Bought and paid for." Jerzy smiled. "Your step-uncle is an opportunist. He saw one. In you."

Jerzy looked down at Elena. A defiant one. Ahh, the art. How to keep her on the edge. Just give her enough to obey and need it, but not enough to make her look like a junky. This one was worth a lot.

"Give me your arm," said Jerzy.

Elena held her arms tightly around her, but though of how good she could feel. Her thoughts turned to Sanja, conjuring an image of her. Was she forgetting what she looked like?

"Give me your arm, or you'll spend three days in the bed," said Jerzy. "I promise. I will let every sick animal have you until you die," he said. Jerzy leaned close to Elena's ear. "And after you die, I will kill your daughter."

Elena's head jerked up and she looked at Jerzy. Jerzy laughed.

"Do you not think I know who your family is? Your father. Your daughter?" he said. "Give me your arm."

Elena held the image of Sanja and offered her arm. Jerzy shot her up, and Elena started to float, the vague image of Sanja melding with a cloud.

"Take off your robe," said Jerzy.

Elena didn't respond, off on the cloud, floating over green hills.

Jerzy untied the robe, opened it and slid it off Elena.

"So very nice."

Jerzy unzipped his pants, exposing himself. "Show me what you can do," he said.

"No please," said Elena, slowly.

"Go to work. Remember what I can do to your daughter. What is her name? Sanja?" he said.

Do what you have to do...to survive, ran through her head, anything to get back to Sanja. She went down.

Jerzy moaned slightly. "Not bad," he said. "But you have a lot to learn. Miri will teach you."

He held the back of Elena's head, causing her to gag. He finished.

"Clean up," said Jerzy. "You have a customer in ten minutes." He looked at Miri.

"Help her get ready."

CHAPTER 8

Vlad and Lincoln Seal a Deal

Vlad turned right on the corner of Woodward and Warren, across from the Wayne State University bookstore. He pulled right, splashing through a puddle where a tall, well dressed man stood. He put the CTS in park and the door locks popped open. Cletus B. Lincoln, the Mayor's Chief of Security opened the door and got in, raincoat and hat wet from the rain.

"Damn rain," he said. "Been rainin' for three days straight now."

Vlad saw the rain from Lincoln's coat and hat run down on the leather seat, turned his head and watched the road. He pulled out on Woodward and adjusted the windshield wipers.

"Get this," said Lincoln. "Eighth Precinct just executed a bust on the west side. Happened a few hours ago. Got a little over ten pounds of smack."

Vlad ran the numbers in his head, and sometimes they ran together- Deutschmarks, Euros, American dollars...this worked out to around eight hundred thousand U.S. dollars.

"Only one arrest," said Lincoln, looking out the window. "Mayor and the Chief are announcing it tomorrow." Lincoln looked at Vlad. "Funny thing is, our dog ripped those motherfuckers off just last April."

"Our dog?" said Vlad.

"The dude we're going to meet," said Lincoln. "Alanzo."

Vlad eyeballed Lincoln, couldn't help looking at his nose, flat and bent to one side.

"They go in, see," said Lincoln. "They got black tee shirts on. Black pants, too. Dude sent one of his hos to WalMart or some shit like that." Lincoln shifted in his seat. "Wrote DEA on the back with yellow tape." Lincoln laughed. "They bust open the door, ripped them off right there," he said. "Shot 'em in the legs, just to make a point." Lincoln sat back. "Big time smack on that job, and got about twenty ounces of coke. About two hundred k's worth. Got some guns, too. Couple of forty fives and an AK-47."

"Kalashnikov," said Vlad.

"Whatever, man," said Lincoln.

They drove north on Woodward, turned right on Bethune then pulled into a deserted parking lot by John R and Smith. Alanzo Hendricks watched the black CTS pull up. Vlad pulled next to Alanzo's ivory Land Cruiser and killed the ignition and headlights.

Funky looking pair, one big white dude, as white as clean snow, the other jet black with a bent nose. He and Lincoln went back, but this other dude. This white dude...

White people were an asset though, if you looked at it like a businessman. Especially out a little farther north, around Seven Mile Road, closer to John R. Go back of any party store, any alley, see white kids shooting up, snorting coke, crack, meth, the works. Hit it right there in the alley. Rich kids. Mommy and Daddy working at their big jobs, kids got time and money to burn and come down for a thrill. Alanzo's there to supply. A little outside the normal system, but this was on the fringe of the city.

Not happy about the protocol, Alanzo got out of the Land Cruiser and got in the back of the CTS. They should have come to his vehicle, especially in the rain. Show a little respect. But going to theirs had its advantages. He was in a defensible position, sitting in back. He opened the door behind Vlad and in got and said, "what's so fucking important that I have to come out here?"

Lincoln turned toward him. "Sorry about the inconvenience. We just wanted to give you the first opportunity with a major hookup."

"Hookup for what?" said Alanzo.

"Some good shit comin' in, my man," said Lincoln. "Grade A, straight from Afghanistan."

Alanzo stared at Lincoln. "That so? What's it got to do with me?"

Lincoln adjusted himself in his seat. "I'm thinking we could work out a deal. I know the Italians would love to get their hands on this." Lincoln shifted position, facing Vlad. "My man here has the hookup." He turned back to Alanzo. "We get it here, you distribute."

"How do I know your shit is any good?" said Alanzo.

"Oh, it's good alright," said Lincoln, looking at Vlad. Vlad pulled a small, waxy packet from his suit coat pocket and handed it to Alanzo. "Check it," said Lincoln. Alanzo opened the packet, dabbed his little finger into the powder, licked it and rubbed some on his gums. After a moment he looked at Lincoln and Vlad and nodded.

"Mind if I take this with me?" he said.

Vlad and Lincoln looked at each other. Lincoln smiled.

"It's all yours."

"So what's your plan?" asked Alanzo.

Lincoln looked at Vlad. Vlad held up his left hand. "First, to show good faith, I will give you half a kilo to distribute. Get the product in the market. Create demand."

Alanzo stared at him. "You mean you'll give me a pound? Just like that?" said Alanzo. He thought for a moment and said, "That's about forty grand."

Vlad shrugged. "To show good faith. I will get the rest here, no problem."

Alanzo sat back. "Man, it ain't so easy bringin' shit in, nowadays, 'specially getting it through the border," he said. "Comin' in from Canada? Less risky than Mexico, but the bridge and tunnel are pretty well covered. Boats and river being monitored by cameras. New shit every day."

"Who said anything about the bridge and tunnel?" said Lincoln.

"How you gonna do it then?" said Alanzo.

"You're asking too many questions," said Lincoln. "Just leave it to us."

Alanzo thought for a moment. "So when you get the first load?" he said.

Lincoln looked at Vlad. "We need a distributor first, with some cash up front," he said. He turned to Alanzo. "You first class all the way, but like I said, there's always the Italians."

"Man, why you keep bringing up the motherfucking Italians?" said Alanzo, agitated. "They done. Chump change. They had their day.

Now let's get down to business. How much can you give me, bitch?"

Lincoln sat up, then softened. This was just business. "Seventy five pounds," he said calmly, looking to Vlad for acknowledgement. Vlad nodded. "That's pure shit, uncut. We figure street value of about seven point two," said Lincoln.

"Seventy five pounds," said Alanzo. "No shit." He made a few quick mental calculations.

"We want sixty percent," said Vlad. He looked Alanzo directly in the eye.

"That's a lot of money," said Alanzo, poker-faced. "I got to think about it."

"Don't think too long," said Lincoln.

"Forty percent," countered Alanzo.

Vlad looked at Lincoln, then at Alanzo. "Fifty."

"All right, man. We got a deal," said Alanzo.

"With two fifty up front," said Vlad. "By next week. I will put up the same."

"Two fifty," said Alanzo, trailing off. "That's a lot of scratch."

"That's what we need," said Lincoln. "Good faith on both sides. You know me. I ain't going nowhere. You always know where to find me."

Alanzo thought a moment then said, "Done."

Vlad leaned forward and held out his hand. "Where I am from, a handshake is an important thing."

Alanzo shrugged and held out his hand. Vlad shook it.

Lincoln smiled. "We'll be in touch. Let me know where we can pick up the two fifty."

Alanzo stepped out of the CTS into the rain, got in the Land Cruiser and drove away.

"Man, live in Detroit," said Lincoln, "Drive an American car. That's what I say."

He looked at Vlad. "I wanted to mention, I got a little party comin' up. With someone important."

"So?" said Vlad.

"I need some of the bitches you run with," said Lincoln.

"Bitches," said Vlad. "How come all my women are bitches? Don't you like?" said Vlad.

"Oh I like," said Lincoln.

What do you need?" said Vlad.

"Two," said Lincoln.

"These girls are very expensive," said Vlad.

"I'm sure we can work something out," said Lincoln. "Got to be first class all the way."

CHAPTER 9

Eddie's In

When he finished, Eddie gripped the metal bar with one hand, lifted himself up, pulled at his gray sweats with his other hand and slid back into the wheelchair. Getting his pants back up was the tough part. Maybe he could come up with something motorized in the short term to move back and forth, like some kind of lift, have Clarence fabricate it. Who would think taking a shit would be such an ordeal.

A slug from an AK-47 in the base of Eddie's spine decided that for him on April 1, 1970. In Vietnam, when he was nineteen years old made it an ordeal...

...Eddie sat with his buddy in front of the black and white television, December 1st, 1969, watching the CBS Special Report on the draft lottery, the announcer saying, "Due to the special report that follows, Mayberry RFD will not be presented tonight"...

Eddie's buddy didn't go to college and was fair

game. So was Eddie, dropping his student deferment. His mother was hysterical. "How can you not stay in college? How can you ruin your life like this? Do you know what can happen?" she said, pacing around the living room the night before, pulling at her hair. "Jewish boys go to college, not to war," she kept repeating.

Eddie didn't give a shit about college, but the problem was, if you didn't go to college in 1969 chances are you were headed to Viet Nam via the draft lottery.

Eddie sat on the floor with his back against a sofa, watching the big RCA television, drinking a bottle of 7-Up. A bunch of old men in suits stood around with some sitting schoolmarm looking woman wearing horn-rimmed glasses. One old guy was introduced and pulled out the first blue plastic pill-like container from a large glass bowl. The container looked like a giant Viagra pill. He opened the container, pulled out a tag with a birthdate printed on it and called out, "September fourteenth, number zero zero one." He handed off the tag, smiled and shook hands with another smiling suit.

SHIT..SHIT..SHIT

It hit Eddie like an incoming missile. He was number one in the draft, and all he wanted to do was to listen to Jimi Hendrix, learn how to play guitar, smoke a little weed here and there and work in the old man's shop, learn the business. He looked at the televised board, 001 on the left, a cream colored card with Sep 14 printed on it, and 018 on the right. The letter from the Draft Board came two weeks later…

Eddie wheeled over to the table with the computer. Funny thing was, even though he couldn't feel a thing from the waist down, he was still horny as hell and loved women. Loved the way they looked, smelled and tasted- all of it. Lap dances, girls straddling him in his wheelchair, naked, rubbing their tits in his face.

Even though his equipment wasn't working, he still got off in his mind. Strippers loved taking care of him. Kind of mothered him. Gave him special treatment, especially at the Tiger's Den. So much so he quit going to other places along Eight Mile. He'd roll up in his modified van, exit via the hydraulic lift and wheel in the front door like a VIP. The girls would see him and come right over, one, two at a time. Vlad took good care of him there.

Man, it wasn't over yet. Chinese stem cell treatment. He read about it, studied it all the time. Read about the guy who was a quadriplegic and could feel his arms again. Read about the guy who could move his legs again, and feel his skin. Fetal brain tissue injections, umbilical chord blood injections. Read the success stories, didn't care about the risks. The Chinese clinics were all over the Web.

Takes time and money. Lots of both, and Eddie was short on money. With enough he could live in China up to six months for treatment and therapy, maybe even a year. Cut this place loose, get treatment then retire somewhere warm, maybe Thailand. Cheap to live, lots of foxy women who did what they were paid to do, and money went far there. This place wasn't worth anything. Did okay with his old man in his day, always broke even during the worst of times, but this was Twenty First Century Detroit, and worth next to nothing. Had some scratch tucked away, about three hundred thousand. With double that amount he could convert the three hundred to diamonds. Not as good as gold, but much more portable. Better than cash. Just one call to the fence and it would happen.

Eddie saw Vlad pull in the yard through the front office window. Eddie felt a pang, yearning as Vlad got out of the CTS and stood. Standing, walking. What was that like? Once in a while it came back to him in dreams, walking as a kid, or running through the elephant grass in Nam. Most of the time it was distant, abstract.

Spend time in China, get fixed and maybe learn to walk again. He was going to be upfront with the Chinese. Walking would be great, but man, the main thing was just to feel his dick again. No matter what it cost and what it took.

Vlad carried a paper bag and knocked. Eddie wheeled to the front entrance and unlocked the steel door. Vlad stood, looking down at Eddie, then walked in. He went over to Eddie's big work table and put down the package.

"Get the glasses. We need to talk some business."

Vlad sat at the work table. Eddie wheeled over to a cabinet and pulled out two filmy shot glasses. Vlad pulled a bottle of Absolut from the bag and poured two shots.

"What's on your mind?" said Eddie.

Vlad smiled. "I have something coming in I need to store. Some packages," he said. "Safely and quietly, and I want access to them when I need."

"Do I get to ask what it is?" said Eddie.

"I would prefer you not," said Vlad.

"You want me to store something, but won't tell me what it is…" said Eddie. "How big is it?"

Vlad shrugged. "Not that big. Thirty four kilos. In ten packages. Around seventy five pounds."

Gotta be coke, or smack, Eddie thought.

"Seventy five pounds?" said Eddie. "Why not keep it at your club?"

"It's best that I keep it somewhere different. Somewhere- unexpected. Somewhere where I can get at it without any trouble, and no extra eyes," said Vlad.

Eddie gripped the arms of the wheelchair. "Look, if we're gonna do business, be straight with me. Or we can't do anything." He looked straight at Vlad. "Packages that size, gotta be coke or smack."

Vlad leaned forward. "The latter," he said.

Eddie nodded his head. "What's in it for me?"

Vlad sat back and smiled. "Four hundred."

Eddie held his poker face. Seventy five pounds, what was that much heroin worth? Wasn't sure, but if Vlad was offering that much to hold it, it had to be worth a lot more. He'd look it up on the Web.

Eddie shook his head no. "It's risky," he said. "Very risky."

"Life is risky," said Vlad. He lifted the shot glass, downed the vodka, and poured another. "You know my father used to make vodka," he said, pronouncing it "wodka". "Out of potatoes. Strong stuff."

"I bet," said Eddie. He downed his shot. He swallowed and the top of his body shook, a mild alcohol induced tremor after the vodka hit his stomach. His lower torso was motionless and felt nothing. "Truth is, I got something I wanna try. Maybe get my life back." Eddie shifted in his chair. "Shit, life back. More like get a few years of a life I never had," he said, slapping his arms up and down on the wheelchair. "I don't know if I can take another year in this chair, let alone whatever time I got left." He looked up at Vlad. "You ever heard of stem cells?"

"Stem cells?" said Vlad. "I have heard of them."

"Seventy five pounds of horse," said Eddie. "That's the rest of my life in jail for possession."

Vlad gestured around the dingy shop. "Or the rest of your life here. In your chair."

Eddie rolled back in the wheelchair. "I've been here thirty five years," he said, looking around the shop. "And what's it got me?" He rolled forward, closer to Vlad. "Seven hundred and fifty," said Eddie.

Vlad shook his head. "Six fifty."

"Seven hundred," said Eddie. "Final offer."

Vlad sat back in his chair. "You know," he said. "The girls, they miss you."

Eddie's serious look softened. He laughed. "I bet they do."

"I will have some new ones soon, I think. Freshen the stable," said Vlad. "Always good to do from time to time."

"That never hurts," said Eddie.

Vlad sighed. "Seven hundred it is. So, do we have a deal?"

"We got a deal," said Eddie.

Vlad reached out and shook Eddie's hand and looked at him in the eyes. "You know, where I come from a handshake is the most important thing. More than a piece of paper. More than a promise. It is a man's honor, and a man's honor is his life."

"I can understand that," said Eddie.

Vlad let go of his hand.

"Seventy five pounds," said Eddie. "I got the perfect place to keep it." He rolled over to a medium size plywood box, near the desk.

"Underneath the box is a floor safe. If you move the box, you can see it."

Vlad stood up and walked over to the box. Even though the box was heavy, he slid it out of the way with one hand, revealing a rectangular false floor.

"Grab a screwdriver and wedge up the floor," said Eddie. Vlad wedged the screwdriver in the false floor outline and pried it up, revealing a large safe.

Eddie rolled over to his desk, got a notepad and stripped off a piece. "Here's the combination. I'll write it down for you." Eddie wrote down the combination and handed it to Vlad. "You can try it if you like."

Vlad took the piece of paper, twirled the combination lock a few times and pulled opened the safe door.

"Smell this place?" said Eddie, looking around the shop. "Oil and solvent. Fucks up a dog's nose. Old man used to keep one around, to protect the yard. After a while the thing couldn't smell for shit. Ran into the same thing in Nam. Dogs used to smell for Charlie piss in the field. The ammonia. If they hung around the motor pool too long, they were useless." Eddie looked at Vlad and smiled. "All I gotta do is line the rim of the safe with axle grease. If they try to pop us, drug sniffing dog won't smell shit."

Vlad nodded. He shut the safe, spun the lock and slid the box back in place.

"I never asked," he said. "What happened to you?"

Eddie wheeled back and looked down.

"Viet Nam," he said. "Took one in the back from an AK-47."

"Kalishnikov," said Vlad.

"Slug's still in there," said Eddie. "Army doctors wouldn't take it out. Too risky, said it could kill me." Eddie rolled over to the hidden safe. "The Chinese doctors can take it out and fix the connections in my spine. Stem cells, man. Stem cells."

* *

After Vlad left, Eddie made a call to his fence to convert the three hundred k he had to cut diamonds.

CHAPTER 10

Martin Green at the Tiger's Den

Martin Green hung outside the Tiger's Den, just out of sight in the darkness, looking at the front door. Used to panhandle around the front door and parking lot, hitting up whoever came near, being polite, saying "Sir, sir?" Following them to their cars. Three kinds- ones that gave money, ones that didn't, and ones that got nasty. Didn't matter. All were worth a shot.

Tried to go inside a couple of times, but didn't make it past the bouncer at the front door. Heard the music, caught a glimpse of a girl on stage, guys stuffing bills into her g-string. The bouncer with the funny accent grabbed him by the collar, dragged him through the parking lot and threw him into the street. Told him the second time if he tried to come in again he would break his legs.

No panhandling today. No more "Sir, sir," thanks to the loaded 38 he found in a garbage can near the corner of Eight Mile and Dequindre.

The dudes in there had money. They might

have less when they came out, but they still had some.

* *

Vlad was on his cell phone in the back office when the bouncer poked his head in the door. Vlad waved him in. He took the phone from his ear and held his other hand over the microphone. "What is it?" he said.

The bouncer motioned toward the direction of the parking lot.

"The little beggar," he said. "He is back."

Vlad put the phone to his ear. "I will call you back," he said. He listened for a moment and said, "Okay, Lamtumire."

Vlad snapped the phone shut and looked at the bouncer.

"Where?"

"Parking lot," said the bouncer. "Do you want me to handle?"

"Not this time," said Vlad. He stood and walked over to an aluminum Louisville Slugger softball bat propped in a corner by the brown leather couch. He picked it up, tapped the barrel in the palm of his hand and said, "Get the car ready."

* *

Martin was too close to the lights in the parking lot. He shuffled to the back of a green dumpster near the cinderblock retaining wall and crouched down, holding the 38. It felt good in his hand. Felt....powerful.

Two men walked out the front door, one tall and one short, laughing. One of them wobbled, then stumbled. Martin took a quick look around, gripped the 38 and walked toward them. He stopped in front of the tall guy. Martin pointed the gun at him and said, "Gimme your wallet."

The two guys looked at each other, then at the 38.

"I said gimme your wallet, goddamn it," said Martin. The 38 shook in his hand.

The two guys ducked, waving their arms in front of their heads.

"Whoa," said the tall guy. "Wait a minute, okay?" The tall guy reached around, pulled out his wallet and held it out. "Here, take it."

Martin stared at the wallet. "Just drop it on the ground." He looked at the short guy who had his hands in the air. "You too."

The short guy reached around to his back pocket. As he pulled his wallet out he saw a giant in a track suit walk up behind Martin and slam him in the ribs with a baseball bat. The 38 flew out of Martin's hand. He made a small, short squawking sound and fell to the ground, wrapping himself in his arms, his legs making crawling motions against the rough asphalt.

"Pick up your wallets," said Vlad. He stood over Martin and looked down at him.

"Holy shit," said the short guy. He and the tall guy picked up their wallets.

"Gentlemen, I apologize," said Vlad.

"Shouldn't we call the cops?" said the tall guy.

"No," said the short guy. "Cindy doesn't know I'm here. If she finds out I've been spending money at tittie bars again, I'm dead," he said. "She'll leave. This time for real."

"Don't worry," said Vlad. "I will take care of this."

Martin let out a cry and gasped for air. Vlad

faced the two men. "Come back again. See the man at the door," he said. "Tell him the boss said for you to have special treatment. On the house." Vlad smiled then turned and looked down at Martin. "Forget this. Now go."

"Okay, man. Whatever you say," said the tall guy. The two men got in their car, backed out, drove through the parking lot and turned onto Eight Mile Road. The short guy in the passenger seat looked back and in the shadows saw Vlad standing over Martin.

Vlad tapped Martin in the head with the bat. It had been awhile. He was going to enjoy himself. The bouncer pulled up in a nondescript black Ford Taurus and popped open the trunk. Vlad hit Martin in the head hard enough to knock him out, but not do any severe damage. He wanted him awake and alert when the time was right.

* *

Martin came to, arms and legs tied to a wooden chair, his mouth gagged with a filthy strip of cotton bed sheet. He blinked and tried to hold his hands to his head but they wouldn't move. Martin pulled at the ropes, but every exertion caused his head to throb.

Vlad circled him. Martin looked up and followed him slowly with his eyes.

"You try to come in my club when you are told to leave," said Vlad, circling slowly. "Then, you try to rob my customers. In my parking lot. At my club."

Vlad stopped in front of Martin's face.

"Very bad for business," said Vlad. "And for you." He pulled a pair of wire cutters from his back pocket. "You know, in some countries they cut off a thief's hands." Vlad held the cutters in front of Martin's face and snapped them open and shut. "I think you will learn a better lesson this way."

Martin's eyes widened and he shook his head from side to side, jumping in the chair. Vlad held down Martin's left hand and cut off his thumb, hearing the gristle pop and the bone snap. Martin screamed through the gag, then let out a succession of long sobs. Vlad quickly held down Martin's other hand and cut off Martin's right thumb.

Vlad held up the thumb so Martin could see it.

"Now, you can no longer hold a gun," said Vlad.

Martin moaned through the gag.

"But still," said Vlad. "Maybe a knife?" Vlad held down Martin's right hand. Martin looked down at his mangled hand, looked at Vlad, made noise and shook his head.

"Do you have something to say?"

Martin shook his head up and down.

Vlad pulled the dirty rag from Martin's mouth. Martin's head dropped, spittle running down his chin. "Please," he whispered.

"Have you learned your lesson?" said Vlad.

"Please...yes," said Martin.

"Will you ever try to steal from my customers again?" said Vlad.

"No," said Martin. "Never. Please...."

Vlad looked down at him, and held down Martin's right hand. "I want to make sure" he said. Vlad quickly cut off the four fingers on Martin's right hand, starting with the index finger. Martin screamed. Vlad was amused at the power behind the outcry, coming from such a little man. The fingers dropped to the floor, one by one. Martin moaned, on the shore of unconsciousness, his head hanging.

Vlad leaned down in front of Martin and held Martin's head up by the chin.

"Will you ever come near my club again?" said Vlad

"No," whispered Martin, weeping. "Never. Never. I swear."

Vlad pulled back his hand and Martin's head dropped. He walked behind Martin.

"I don't believe you," he said.

Vlad picked up a plastic two liter pop bottle filled with gasoline and poured half of it on Martin and the rest on the dry wooden floor around him. Martin's head popped up. He choked on the gasoline and flailed his head. The gasoline brought the burning, electric pain back in his hands.

Vlad opened a book of matches, lit them, and threw them at Martin's feet. The gas instantly ignited, covering Martin in an orange fireball. Martin screamed, struggled in the chair, bubbled, then blackened and went still. The old floorboards caught fire and quickly spread. Vlad walked down the stairs, crushing broken hypodermic needles under his boots and strolled out the door. He got in the passenger's seat of the Taurus and nodded to the bouncer at the wheel. Great car for these little projects. So many on the road, and they all look alike. The bouncer and Vlad drove away, smoke now pouring from the windowless house.

Over eighty thousand abandoned houses in this city. Pick one, do your work, burn it down. No one snitches.

CHAPTER 11

Chris Picks Up a Fare

Chris sat in the limo in the parking lot by the RiverWalk, in view of the carousel, Caesar's Casino on the Windsor side and the Renaissance Center on the right. It wasn't really a limo, but a bubbly black Lincoln Town Car. Chris loosened his tie. He didn't mind wearing the chauffeurs suit, simple and black, but he hated the hat that the limo company made him wear. And he also had to shave.

The parking lot was empty and there wasn't much business this time of morning, which Chris didn't mind. He looked at the idle carousel and saw a solitary black guy fishing, right where the RiverWalk ended and the State Park began. Die hard. Some guys fish no matter what time of year or weather. Probably fishing for muskie. Chris saw the guy set his jig and deftly cast it in the water. He obviously knew how to fish.

A freighter slipped by going upstream toward Lake St. Claire. A couple more months and the river would be filled with giant ice floes, jammed together like giant blue-green pieces of mismatched linoleum.

A siren sounded in the distance. Chris half smiled. One thing about Detroit, there were always sirens, as constant as the river current. He got out of the Town Car, leaned against the front left fender and lit a cigarette. Against the rules, but fuck it.

He took a drag off the cigarette and saw a large, white yacht emerge from the Belle Isle shipping channel. Just like the TradeWind, a Hatteras Convertible. White and sleek, but in a classic way. Flying bridge, easily rigged for fishing or cruising. Chris figured it to be a fifty two- same length as the TradeWind. He stared at the boat as it passed and thought he better call the marina this week to see if anyone inquired about the TradeWind. Sure, there were a lot of boats available, but this one stuck to him. Perfect spot, the little Key Cove Marina, small and personal. Chris felt lucky the guy that owned the boat liked him and said that he would hold off selling it and give Chris first shot. He said Chris could take over his steady Marlin charter, too. Introduce him to his steady clients. It was perfect.

He could live on the boat, in the smaller state room and leave the main quarters for the clients if they stayed out overnight. A great little galley, too. He'd be done with this life, the limo, Eddie's chop shop, and Detroit. Problem was, the guy who owned the TradeWind was getting ready to retire, six months maybe, and as Chris figured it, he needed at least another year to come up with the rest of the cash. He watched the Hatteras motor downriver with the current, passing in front of the RenCen toward the bend in the river under the

Ambassador Bridge. He had to call the guy, tell him things were going good. Reassure him that he'd come up with the cash, soon.

Chris's pager lit up, displaying a code. A pickup in front of the Wintergarden. An airport run. He stamped out his cigarette and got in the limo. Chris straightened his tie and put on his cap, avoiding looking at himself in the mirror.

Chris pulled out of the lot onto Atwater and headed toward the RenCen. He passed by the near empty parking structure on Beaubien and slowed as he approached the Wintergarden doors. An attendant flagged him down. Next to him stood a large man in a royal blue tracksuit.

Vlad's head reared back when he recognized Chris. The attendant put Vlad's suitcase in the Town Car's trunk and held open the rear door. Vlad got in and sat back, amused, looking at Chris in the rearview mirror. Chris waited for a pedestrian to cross, then pulled onto Atwater.

"I did not know you were a taxi driver," said Vlad.

Chris kept his eyes on the road. "This is a limo. Not a taxi."

"So it is," said Vlad. "So, mister limo driver, why do you do this?"

Chris shrugged. "Day gig, part time. Gotta have some kind of job, for taxes. And cover."

Vlad considered this. "Maybe you could come work for me."

Chris looked at Vlad in the rear view mirror. "And do what?"

"I can think of many things," said Vlad. He looked out the window. "You know, your friend Eddie comes into my club. Quite often. He's told me a lot about you."

Chris frowned. Fuckin' Eddie. "And what did

he say?" said Chris.

"How you came to him. How he likes you. How you work," said Vlad.

Chris nodded, wondering where this was leading, getting more pissed off at Eddie by the minute.

"He also says he never saw you with a girl," said Vlad.

"So?"

"Don't you like girls?"

"Sure I do."

"So why no women? No girlfriend?"

"What's with the personal questions?"

Vlad stared out the window. Chris pulled onto I-375 toward I-94 and the airport.

"Why don't I have a girlfriend?" said Chris. "Too much baggage. Don't have the time. There's certain things I want. End of story."

Vlad leaned forward. "And what is it you want?"

Chris smiled. "That's my business."

Vlad leaned back. "You know, my father was a fisherman," he said. "Worked on a trawler. Baltic Sea. A healthy life. It would have been much better for him if he had owned his own boat, don't you think?"

Chris's face turned red. Eddie the asshole, can't keep his mouth shut.

"Florida is very nice," said Vlad, looking out the window at the big Goodyear tire on I-94.

Chris gripped the steering wheel and changed lanes. "Yes it is," he said. He drove smoothly through traffic, got off on Merriman road and cruised up to the International Terminal. He got out of the car and pulled Vlad's bag from the trunk. Vlad didn't wait for Chris to come around and open the door.

"What do I owe you?" asked Vlad.

Chris looked up at him. Man, this dude was big. "Seventy five," he said.

Vlad handed Chris two hundred dollar bills. "You come with Eddie to my club when I return. Meet some girls, maybe talk some business." Vlad waved off a porter and picked up his bag. He leaned down and said, "You could be in that boat sooner than you think." Not waiting for a response Vlad turned and walked toward the terminal doors.

CHAPTER 12

Washington and Peabody Case the Tiger's Den

Ann Peabody sat at the small conference room table in the Bunker, waiting for Washington. She was swiping her tablet computer, examining a street level view of the Tiger's Den. Cement gray with a pink awning and an orange neon sign that said Tiger's Den over an orange and black tigress, ready to pounce. Washington walked in carrying a cup of coffee. Peabody looked up at him.

"You're late," she said.

Washington looked at her squarely in the eyes and said, "Look, I've been assigned to help you, and I'll do that." He leaned over the table. "But if you think I'm going to take any shit from you, you're sadly mistaken." Washington stood straight. "Now," he said. "Would you like to start over?"

Peabody looked up at Washington and smiled.

"You're still late. Come around and take a look," she said, swiping at the tablet. She brought up a report with Vlad's picture in the upper right corner. "Looks like our guy's flown to Athens," said Peabody, conjuring an image of a boarding pass. "My guess is that he'll pick up a flight to Tirana. Cheap. Costs about eighty eight euros," she said.

Washington looked down at the tablet while Peabody swiped back to the Tiger's Den.

"Let's go for a ride," she said.

* *

Washington drove north on Woodward toward Eight Mile, the dividing line between Detroit and the suburbs.

"You know there's a wall here, divides Detroit from the suburbs," said Washington. "Along Eight Mile. Black folk try and move in, every white person would sell and head farther away. All directions, but especially north. White folks finally had enough and put up a wall." He looked at Peabody. "It's a half mile long, intersection at Wyoming. Our own little Berlin wall, right here in Detroit." Washington looked at the road. "Insurance companies wouldn't cover houses in mixed neighborhoods."

"I didn't know that," said Peabody.

"So how did you wind up in Detroit?" said Washington.

Peabody shrugged. "They move us around a lot," she said. "Standard rotation."

Washington stopped at a red light just north of I-94. He stopped with enough distance between them and the car ahead so he could see the bottom of the rear tires. That way if he had to make a quick run for it there was plenty of room to maneuver. He'd been jacked once, and once was enough. Shot and killed the unarmed dude and got suspended for eight weeks pending the outcome of the investigation. Earned the rep as being trigger happy, and it cost him and the city. Now stopping short was SOP, Standard Operating Procedure.

"I've been working on this case for awhile," said Peabody.

"How long have you been DEA?" asked Washington.

"Seven years," said Peabody. "Went to law school. Worked on Wall Street for awhile. Hated it, but it paid off my student loan."

"Law school," said Washington. "Where at?"

"Cornell," said Peabody. "Ithaca, New York. Hometown."

Washington nodded. Cornell. The light turned green and Washington moved forward.

"What about you?"

"Long story," said Washington. "Went to Wayne State, right here in Detroit. Political science, pre-law. Wanted to go to law school."

"What happened?" said Peabody.

Washington shrugged. "Got married, had a kid. Had a buddy who joined the DPD." He looked at Peabody. "Just followed him in and never looked back. We became partners after a couple years."

Washington changed lanes. Peabody looked out the window at the large, once stately houses with large lots and ancient trees. "These must have been beautiful once," she said.

"They were back in the day, I imagine," said Washington. "Detroit in the early twentieth century was the manufacturing equivalent of Silicon Valley. Innovation everywhere. Henry Ford, five dollars a day, all that."

Washington braked for a stray dog crossing the street. "People came from all over the country to work," he said. "The world, for that matter. My father came up from Alabama."

Peabody looked at a windowless, burned out home. "And the rest is history?"

"Who knows?" said Washington. "Maybe this city is a victim of itself. The world changed, and we turned a blind eye to it," he said. "People started buying Japanese cars, 'cause they were better. We didn't wake up until it was too late."

They passed the adult bookstores on the corner of Six Mile and Woodward, where the road expanded from two lanes to six.

"A lot of hard working people here, though," said Washington. "My old man worked at the Rouge Plant. Thirty six years. Could have gone thirty and out, but stayed on another six to put us through school," he said. He looked at Peabody. "Never wanted us to work there. Anywhere but on the line."

Peabody nodded.

Washington cleared his throat. "One thing bothers me, I gottta say," he said.

"What's that?" said Peabody.

"I don't like it when you people let things walk," said Washington. "Especially guns."

Peabody looked at him, surprised at the rapid change of subject. "You people?" she said.

"You know what I mean," said Washington.

"That's ATF," she said. "Occasionally DEA. Same with informants. SOP, just like you." Peabody glanced at the road. "Let a little fish go, maybe lead to a bigger one. Let ten guns go, maybe capture a hundred." Peabody's voice trailed off.

Washington shook his head. "I'll go for the bust," he said. "A bird in hand…"

"If it's anything to you," said Peabody.

"Someone close to me was killed by a gun that walked. A border patrol agent. Picked off just like that. In Mexico. Juarez, across from El Paso."

"Man," said Washington. "I'm sorry to hear that."

They cruised past Seven Mile Road and turned right onto Eight Mile, driving past the abandoned State Fair Grounds. Washington drove for a mile or so then slowed.

"There it is," said Peabody, looking at the neon sign with the painted tiger below. "Have you ever been inside?"

"In there?" said Washington. He pulled onto a side street and stopped in view of the club. "No. I'm not Vice and I'm not a strip club kind of guy."

"You are now," said Peabody.

They sat and watched the club, scanning the parking lot, dumpster and alley in the rear.

"We need to get inside," said Peabody. "Look around. A lot of places have amateur night."

Washington looked at her.

"Surprised?" said Peabody. She looked at the club. "I can handle myself on one of those poles."

They watched the club for another fifteen minutes. Four cars in the parking lot, one large Dodge van with a handicapped plate. Washington started the car and as they pulled onto Eight Mile Peabody saw a diminutive, graying man in a wheelchair roll out the front door, held open by a bouncer.

CHAPTER 13

Concrete Mushrooms

The money, hidden in a crate full of spark plugs, left the Port of Detroit and arrived in Toulon, France eight days later. From there the box was driven to Milan and uncrated at a social club. The money was placed in two canvass duffel bags and driven down the coast to Bari. The bags were handed off to two men who boarded a daily ferry that went across the Adriatic to Durres, Albania. The money was on shore and hidden as Vlad looked down at Athens from a first class window seat.

He cleared customs and boarded a flight from Athens to Tirana. After less than an hour the small jet touched down at Rinas International. He walked out of the customs booth looking as fresh as when he left Detroit, twelve hours earlier.

Vlad slung his leather travel bag over his shoulder and spotted a thin, dark man near a coffee stand, smoking a cigarette. They made eye contact. The man butted out his cigarette, turned and started walking toward the terminal exit. Vlad slowed and followed, leaving a gap of at least twenty feet between them.

They boarded a bus that headed north, passed through the empty traffic circle and were dropped off in an open air parking lot. The bus lumbered away and Vlad and the man hugged and kissed each other on the cheek.

"Gregor, my old friend," said Vlad. "Good to see you."

"The pleasure is mine."

They walked to a small sedan. Vlad was amused.

"I am to fit in this?"

"Don't worry," said Gregor. "This is just temporary."

Vlad tossed his bag in the back seat and got in the car, squeezing himself into the passenger's seat. Gregor pulled out of the parking lot and drove south, eventually coming to SH2. They passed Polis University and turned onto Rruga 29. After several miles they took an exit and drove west to a garage. Gregor opened the rusty door then pulled inside. They got into Gregor's Land Rover and drove to the fringe of Tirana, stopping at the safe house.

Vlad and Gregor walked upstairs to a large open space furnished with a workbench, desk, table, camera equipment, two computer workstations and a two color laserjet printers along with assorted boxed of high grade paper and cardboard. Three automatic weapons, ammunition and two 45 caliber pistols were neatly laid out on the workbench. Gregor handed a pistol to Vlad.

In the corner were ten bricks of neatly packed heroin. Thirty four kilograms, each brick containing 3.4 kilos, or a little under seven and a half pounds. Vlad looked at the bricks and smiled.

"Never say Gregor does not deliver," said Gregor.

Vlad nodded.

"Our new route," said Gregor. "It is nearly perfect. Protected. Good political support." Gregor looked at Vlad. "I just need to take care of someone first."

"Can I help?" said Vlad.

Gregor shook his head. "Unnecessary. I will deal with him as soon as we are through. Wants too much and knows too much." Gregor smiled. "Who knows," he said. "I might even send you a picture."

Vlad nodded and looked at the computers and printers. "I may need some passports and papers."

"How many?" said Gregor.

"One, possibly two," said Vlad. "U.S. Female."

Gregor nodded. "How soon?"

"Two, maybe three days," said Vlad. He looked at Gregor. "Is that possible?"

Gregor put his hand to his chin. "That's not much time, but enough. Should not be a problem. Bring them here and I'll see what I can do."

Vlad nodded. "Shall we get down to business?" he said. "I have the distribution arranged. With a certain degree of protection and excellent intelligence."

Gregor nodded. "We expect the flow of cash every two weeks."

"Not a problem," said Vlad. "Detroit is very systematic."

Vlad learned the Detroit system from Cletus B. Lincoln. With twenty thousand addicts, demand was high. Lincoln said to Vlad, "man, they don't sell to junkies in the street here. It's busted up into two gigs." Lincoln went on to say the two gigs were quarter houses and shooting galleries. Dudes that owned shooting galleries came in and bought caps at the quarter houses, which were like wholesalers. Dudes would take the caps back to their shooting galleries and sell hits to their junkies. Make 'em shoot up right there, just to make sure they weren't undercover cops. Plenty of shooting galleries in Detroit- at least two thousand. Lincoln said he knew of twenty on Mack Avenue alone, near Comerica Park. Alanzo Hendricks controlled a lot of the quarter houses in Detroit, along with a number of shooting galleries. Lincoln knew some of Alanzo's galleries brought in at least ten thousand a week, let alone what came into the quarter houses. If up-and-comers got in Alanzo's way, they were executed, plain and simple. Cops had so much other shit to do few q-houses and galleries were busted.

Vlad and Gregor waited until sunset and loaded the heroin in the back of the Land Rover, covering it with a green woolen army blanket. They drove north, past the airport toward the port of Durres.

"You know my uncle," said Vlad. "My mother's brother. Spent eight years in prison for having a map," said Vlad referring to the days under the communist regime when it was illegal to own a map of Albania. "Some good with it, though," he said. "You learn how to get around by landmark only."

"True," said Gregor.

They pulled into Durres and passed by the sparse train station. A vintage cold war diesel locomotive, green, white and burnt orange sat idle on the tracks. They cruised past the ancient Roman amphitheater. Vlad studied it as they rolled by.

"I would have felt very comfortable in there," he said.

"I believe you would," said Gregor. "The dragon in the arena."

They drove along the remote northern coastline, the hillside populated by concrete bunkers, short and toadstool-like. Just a subset of the seven hundred and fifty thousand constructed during the early fifties under the paranoid communist dictatorship, built to fend off an invasion that never materialized. Many were spray painted with graffiti, names of World Cup teams and players.

Vlad looked out the window. "The coast reminds me of my father," he said. "People are such fools. They work. Sacrifice for others, and where does that get them? Nowhere. There is only yourself."

Gregor switched the Land Rover into four wheel drive, killed the headlights and pulled off the gravel road. He navigated up a hill and stopped near a derelict bunker surrounded by tall grass and brush.

"Concrete mushrooms," said Gregor. "Very useful."

Vlad and Gregor got out of the Land Rover and walked to the bunker. Vlad reached inside the rectangular aperture, down toward the false floor, touched a bag and felt for the canvass handle. He pulled out the bag and handed it to Gregor. He reached in and pulled out the second bag. They unzipped the bags, revealing neatly bound packets of one hundred dollar bills.

They zipped up the bags and loaded the bricks of heroin.

"They will be out of here and on their way by

morning," said Gregor.

Vlad and Gregor were getting in the Land Rover when they heard a twig snap and saw a silhouette moving against the moonlight. The figure stopped and bent over, picked something up, then moved again. Vlad and Gregor looked at each other and pulled their guns. They scrambled up the hill and converged on a young man, maybe eighteen or nineteen years old. He stopped when he saw Vlad and Gregor.

"What are you doing here?" said Vlad.

The young man looked at the guns. "Just getting some firewood."

"Firewood for what?" said Vlad.

"For a fire. My girlfriend and I are camping."

"Where?" said Vlad.

The young man pointed to a hilltop. "Over that ridge, near the beach."

Vlad looked at Gregor, then back at the young man. "Take us there."

"Why?" said the young man. "Are you the police or something? I haven't done anything wrong."

Vlad pointed the gun at the young man's face. "Shut up and take us there."

The young man dropped the wood and started walking up the hill. "What did I do wrong?" he said.

"Just keep moving," said Vlad.

They cleared the hilltop, the moonlight sparking over the Adriatic Sea. A tent was pitched on the beach. A female figure stood next to the tent, outlined against the water.

Vlad, Gregor and the young man walked down to the tent and stopped.

"What's going on?" said the young woman, stunned at seeing her boyfriend with two men holding guns.

"Pack up your tent," said Vlad. "You're coming with us."

"I don't understand," said the young woman.

"Shut up and pack your things," said Vlad.

"But we've done nothing wrong," said the young man.

Vlad swung around and hit him in the side of the jaw with his gun. He dropped to his knees and his girlfriend rushed over to him.

"What are you doing?" she cried. "Why are you doing this?"

"Pack up the tent. Now," said Vlad.

The girlfriend helped the young man up. He stood, dazed for a moment then started taking down the tent. The young woman started crying.

"Please," she said. "We did nothing."

"No talking," said Vlad.

They packed the tent in a nylon carrying case and rolled up two sleeping bags. The young man carried the tent and a sleeping bag. The young woman carried her sleeping bag and a small mess kit.

"Move," said Vlad, pointing to the hilltop.

They walked over the hill, passed the bunker loaded with heroin and headed down the hill toward the Land Rover. Gregor opened the Rover's rear gate.

"Put the tent and bags in here," said Vlad. "You," he said to the young man. "Get in the front." He pointed the gun at the young woman. "You get in the back."

The young man looked at his girlfriend and yelled, "Run!" He charged at Gregor, tackling him. The young woman ran down the hill. Vlad walked over, picked up the young man by the collar and threw him down. He aimed the gun at the back of the young man's head and fired.

The young woman heard the shot, a crack echoing off the hills and let out a sharp cry. Vlad saw her stumble, get up and run toward the road. He held the gun with both hands and aimed. The young woman looked back. Vlad squeezed off a shot, hitting the woman in the nose, the bullet exiting through the back of her skull. She dropped and tumbled a short distance down the hill and stopped.

"Shit," said Vlad. "I didn't want that to happen here. Let's load them and go."

Vlad walked down the hill, grabbed the dead woman by the leg and dragged her up the hill. They could wrap the bodies in the army blanket and dump them in the Adriatic a few miles up the coast, at the point. The current would take them all the way to Greece. A shame. Vlad looked down at the dead woman. She might have done well at the Tiger's Den.

CHAPTER 14

Vinnie the Viper

A cylinder on the Harley wasn't acting right. Missed firing twice. An average rider wouldn't notice it, but Chris did. He was sensitive to every little nuance, every little quirk in the bike's performance and behavior. He rumbled into the ACE garage to check it out.

Eddie sat at the table with Vinnie Tucci with a bottle of Johnny Walker Black between them. At Vinnie's side sat a scowling, tattooed young man maybe about twenty that resembled Vinnie.

"Whoa," said Eddie. "Look who's here."

Vinnie looked at Chris and nodded. "Long time no see."

"Hey Vinnie," said Chris. He looked at the young man.

"Take a seat," said Eddie. "Have a drink with us."

Vinnie put his arm around the young man's shoulder and pulled him in.

"This is my nephew Paulie," he said.

Chris nodded. He sat. "I'll pass on the drink," he said. "I'm driving."

"Hey man. I don't drink that shit either," said Paulie, pointing to the bottle of JWB. "Blue label only."

Vinnie got serious. "I was tellin' Eddie, someone boosted a hauler full of Escalades. Driver worked for a friend of mine." He sat back and downed a shot of JWB. "Get this," he said. "Even had the keys shipped separately. Amateurs would have cut loose right there. Had to be some talent on that job." He looked directly at Eddie. "Hear anything about it?"

Eddie looked Vinnie in the eye and said, "No. Not a word."

Vinnie fixed on Eddie's face. After a moment he sat back.

"Whoever pulled this job should be careful. If you catch wind of anything, do me a favor and let me know."

"They're dead meat," said Paulie.

Vinnie smacked him in the head. "What's wrong with you? Did I tell you to talk?"

Paulie sat back and lit a cigarette.

"Let me put it to you this way," said Vinnie. "Whoever did this isn't a friend of mine. It brings unnecessary heat."

Chris looked at Eddie. "I thought you didn't have any friends, only customers?"

"We got friends," said Eddie, shifting his weight in his wheelchair, "and good ones. Like Vinnie."

Eddie wheeled a little closer to the table, toward Chris. "Vinnie has something for us," he said.

Vinnie chimed in, and said slowly, "big party at the RenCen. The Marriot. Benefit for Detroit

Receiving Hospital. Lots of doctors gonna be there. Rich ones. Always some lawyers, too."

"I know the structure there," said Chris.

"It's not that structure, the one across Beaubien. Some big automotive convention's going on at the same time. Structure's booked solid for two days. Same time as the party. Doctors were pissed. They're parking in the Millender structure. Valets will take the cars from the door."

"I know that structure, too. Low concrete. Narrow and tight. Got to watch your speed or you go airborne and the car's done," said Chris. "So what are we looking for?"

"CL class," said Vinnie. "Top of the list. Then C class. BMW from there."
Chris nodded.

"Want 'em intact, and want at least four, five if you can," said Vinnie. "It goes down two weeks from now. On a Saturday night."

"We'll work on intel," said Eddie.

"You in?" Vinnie said to Chris.

"Sure," said Chris. "What's the take?"

"The usual," said Vinnie, sitting back. "Another thing," he said to Eddie. "You'd be doing me a huge favor if you could take Paulie on. As an apprentice, maybe." He pinched Paulie's cheek. Paulie scowled and pulled away. "Show him the ropes, so to speak. Start him out small, make him work." He looked at Eddie. "Make his mother happy."

After a small flash of surprise, Eddie nodded and said, "sure, shouldn't be a problem, Vinnie. We'll work something out." Eddie looked at Paulie, then Vinnie. "Start next week?"

"Sure thing," said Vinnie. He turned to Paulie. "Thank the man."

"Thanks, man," said Paulie.

"Alright," said Vinnie. He stood. "Adios. Paulie, let's go."

Paulie stood and followed Vinnie out.

* *

After Vinnie and Paulie drove away, Chris said, "What about the Albanian? Vinnie's thinking you're playing both sides of the fence. That's why he's sticking that little greaseball with us."

"Vinnie don't know. He may suspect, but he don't know. And what Vinnie don't know won't hurt him. Or us," said Eddie.

"Bullshit. He'll cut your balls off if he found out. Mine too. You know how he is," said Chris.

"Read my lips," said Eddie. "What Vinnie don't know won't hurt him. Besides, Vlad's into something new. Bigger take."

"You get in deep shit, don't involve me. I don't want to wind up floating down the Detroit River," said Chris.

Eddie looked at Chris. "Bust my balls all you want," he said. "I can't feel them anyway." He rolled back in the wheelchair. "Extra three grand for you if you score a CL."

"Deal," said Chris. His expression turned serious. "How did Vinnie get wind of the Escalades? I thought it was just us that knew? You, me, Clarence, Zippy and Jesus."

"Things get out on the street. You know that," said Eddie.

"Still, I don't like it," said Chris. "What do you know about this Vlad dude, anyway? At least with Vinnie you know where you stand. Besides, you two go back." Chris lit a cigarette and took a deep drag.

"Way back," said Eddie.

Vinnie and Eddie did go back. Humping on patrol in Vietnam. Same unit. Vinnie was vicious in the field, where he picked up the nickname "The Viper," wasting anything that moved while out on patrol. Vinnie was in Nam six months before Eddie. 11-Bravo. Eddie being an FNG-fucking new guy fresh out of jungle school, was ignored by the rest of the unit until he talked to Vinnie and found out he was from Grosse Pointe. "Oak Park Eddie," Vinnie called him. They both were outliers, the Jewish kid from Oak Park and the Mafia punk from Grosse Pointe. They hung out together in the field barracks made of old ammo boxes on a cement slab with a sheet metal roof, eating C rations, some going back to World War II. Vinnie would go after the beans and meatballs and Eddie ate ham and eggs. Far from kosher, but fuck it.

One night in Injun country they got into a firefight outside a village, trapping a squad of VC and wasting them all except for one. They tied him up and sat him down in a clearing surrounded by elephant grass. The Lieutenant had Vinnie carry a bag of onions in a big, sealed plastic bag, just for occasions like this. Something he learned from a South Vietnamese Captain. Vinnie took the onions, cut them up, put them in the bag and put the bag over the gook's head. The onion vapor instantly choked him. The Lieutenant radioed in for an interpreter.

After just over a minute the Lieutenant told Vinnie to remove the onion bag. The prisoner gasped, coughed and refused to talk. They put the bag back over his head and the prisoner collapsed, unconscious. They smacked him in the face to revive him, but he still said nothing. Tough little bastard. The Lieutenant told Vinnie to take the bag of onions and bury it, and told Eddie to go with him. They did and on the way back they heard two pops from an M16.

Khe Sahn came down the next day. Vinnie came out unscathed but Eddie wasn't so lucky. Eddie took two hits from an AK47, one in the shoulder and one near the stomach to the spine, paralyzing him from the waist down. Eddie was completely numb and feeling just fine from morphine as the medevac chopper lifted from the LZ. During surgery the doctors decided to leave the slug in his spine rather than risking more damage.

Eddie spent three months in a Saigon hospital, then six months in a hospital stateside. On discharge he went back to Detroit and went to work at ACE, focusing on running the business, forgetting about Nam and learning to live with his disability.

Nobody gave a shit about returning Vietnam vets. They were considered the enemy also, right along with Johnson and Nixon. Eddie hid in the inner office at ACE, thinking about Nam and women. Never got laid at home. Not by an all-American girl. Sure, he fooled around with some girls in high school, but never the full thing.

On leave he went with Vinnie to a whorehouse in Saigon a couple of times, but GIs were suspicious and wary of hookers. Funny how they said "You like boom-boom? I boom-boom you real good." Most were VC and everyone heard the legends about GIs getting fatal doses of clap and the hookers who stuck razor blades up their snatches.

Eddie looked up at Chris, smoking the cigarette. "Gimme one of those."

"I thought you quit," said Chris.

"New Year's Resolution," said Eddie. "Start smoking again and drink more."

Chris pulled the pack from his pocket, tapped out a smoke and handed it to Eddie.

"Light?" said Eddie.

"Jesus," said Chris. "Smoke it for you too?" He pulled out his old Zippo, flicked it and held it to the cigarette. Eddie lit up.

"You know," said Chris. "The Escalade driver can ID me. What if Vinnie won't let this go? We're fucked, big time."

"That ship has sailed. Vinnie's got bigger fish to fry. We do this Marriot boost and we're gold."

Chris took a drag off his cigarette. "What about this Paulie asshole? You know that's why Vinnie stuck him with you. He doesn't trust you." Chris flicked the cigarette ash on the shop floor. "Where you gonna put this guy, anyway? No way he's with me."

Eddie thought a moment. "I'll put him with Zippy, maybe Clarence."

"Clarence'll kill him," said Chris.

"You're right," said Eddie. "Zippy it is."

* *

Vinnie drove out of Detroit and took the Square Lake exit toward Bloomfield Hills. He turned on Telegraph Road and passed by where the old Red Fox restaurant once stood. One day was fixed in his mind, July 30, 1975. The day he made his bones. The mark really did look like a bulldog. Scheduled to meet Tony Jack and Tony Pro, have lunch, square things.

Didn't happen.

Instead of meeting Tony Jack and Tony Pro,

Vinnie met him with two guys from New York. Told him the big guys didn't want to meet in public, and said they were here to take him to a house in Bloomfield Hills to meet with them. The mark didn't like it and was suspicious, of course, but what could he do? This was the last chance to make things right before everything turned to shit. The mark got in the car, sitting between the two guys from New York. Vinnie drove.

They went to an isolated house near Stony Craft golf course, got out, went inside and one of the New York guys did him right there, in the foyer. Two shots, back of the head with a 38. Vinnie was on cleanup detail, mopping up the blood as fast as possible and bleaching it down while the New York guys wrapped the body in a blanket. Clean, well placed shots. A little brains and blood in a side table, but none on the walls. These guys were good.

They waited until dark. Just so happened they were pouring the foundation for the new Matilda Wilson wing of the Detroit zoo's aviary that night and next day. They just poured one slab a little early, which was no big deal since Vinnie's boss was hooked up with one of the contractors. They took the body to the zoo in a work van, drove to the construction site and put the body and the blanket in the excavation. The mixer was already rolling. They covered the body with concrete and smoothed the slab, the first poured for the new wing.

Now, when families ooh and aah at the exotic birds cruising around the aviary, they have no clue they're walking over Jimmy Hoffa.

CHAPTER 15

Vlad Visits Jerzy

Jerzy Vogodian was stunned when he looked through the peephole and saw the Dragon. "Shit," he said, tapping the bouncer's shoulder. "Open the door, open the door." The bouncer obliged. Vlad was smiling and looking down at an image on his cell phone sent by Gregor.

"Vlad, my old friend," said Jerzy. "I didn't expect to see you so soon." Jerzy stepped aside. "Come in, come in." Vlad flipped his phone shut, stepped in and each man hugged and patted the other on the back both with eyes wide open.

"So what brings you back this time?" asked Jerzy.

"Just some business," said Vlad. "And pleasure." Vlad smiled. "What do you have that's new?"

Jerzy stepped back and tried to recall where Elena was at the moment. After adding the receipts and cash for an hour he forget where she was supposed to be- dancing or with a customer.

Sloppy. He turned and looked around the floor and stage. She must be with a customer. He saw Miri at the bar, smoking a cigarette.

"Not much new," he said. "Business has been slow. I can set you up nicely, though. Follow me."

They walked past the bar and Jerzy snapped his fingers. The bartender pulled a bottle of Absolut and started a setup with two glasses and ice. Jerzy and Vlad walked through the main parlor, passed the stage and entered a private room lined with red velvet wallpaper, furnished with a couch and two oversized blue velvet chairs. Vlad sat on the couch and Jerzy sat in a chair. Techno droned in the background.

Jerzy glanced at the bar and saw the bartender was finished with the tray.

"Let me get our drinks," said Jerzy. Vlad nodded. Jerzy stood and walked to the bar. A naked woman slowly started walking towards Vlad, seeing Jerzy leave.

"Miri, where is Elena," said Jerzy.

Miri studied Jerzy's expression, never seeing him this nervous. "Upstairs with someone."

"Go upstairs. When she is finished tell her to stay there. Out of sight. She is not to come down, understand?"

Miri looked over Jerzy's shoulder and saw Vlad. Vlad looked at her as the naked woman walked up and stood in front of him.

"Go. Tell her now," said Jerzy.

Miri nodded and walked toward the stairs. Jerzy took the tray with the setup and walked briskly back to Vlad. The naked woman looked down at Vlad, swaying side to side, flipping her brown hair. Jerzy motioned for her to leave. She pouted and slowly walked away.

"Just how I remember you," said Vlad. "A

waiter."

Jerzy forced a smile. "Old times," he said. "I would rather forget." He poured the vodka into the glasses, the ice popping. He raised his glass and said "Skoal!"

They were on their second round when Vlad said, "Who was that you were talking to at the bar? The one with the missing finger?"

Jerzy sat back. "She's been here awhile."

Vlad nodded. "She looks interesting."

"She's nothing all that special," said Jerzy.

"The older ones," said Vlad. "They must be exceptional to keep them around. Bring her over."

Jerzy hesitated, then turned and looked toward the bar. He caught Miri's eye and waved her over.

Miri wore a short robe, open with nothing underneath. She walked toward them, one high-heeled foot in front of the other, like a cat. She stopped in front of Vlad.

"Miri, this is my old comrade, Vlad," said Jerzy.

He motioned for her to sit next to Vlad. Miri sat and automatically put her hand on Vlad's inner thigh.

Vlad ignored Miri. "I am looking to purchase." He leaned forward. "What do you have that is new?"

Jerzy shook his head. "Nothing really."

Vlad nodded, took a drink and said, "Any news of the Army lately?"

Jerzy looked at him. "No."

"No? I understand they have been very active. Even around here. Are you sure?"

"Yes, sure," said Jerzy.

"So they have not bothered you?" said Vlad. "That is good, but these times are so uncertain. Unstable. Alliances change so easily, day to day.

You never know what could happen. Who to trust." Vlad reached into his jacket pocket and pulled out his cell phone, opened it and brought up an image on the small screen Gregor had sent him.

"I have something to show you," he said. "I just received this from a very good friend of mine." He leaned forward and turned the phone so Jerzy could see the image. "Here, take a good look."

Jerzy wasn't sure what he was looking at, and then it came together. He saw a bloody, beaten body, it's severed head tucked neatly between the right arm and torso, mouth open, eyes bulging. Jerzy jumped back in his chair, away from the phone.

"Is this a threat?" he said.

"Not at all," said Vlad. "But these things happen from time to time." He flipped the phone shut and put it in his jacket pocket.

Jerzy sat back and closed his eyes for a moment. Then he said, "Miri, go get Elena."

Miri nodded. "I think she is with a customer."

Jerzy flashed an angry look. "Do it. Now."

Miri got up, walked to the stairway and scrambled up the stairs. A few moments later Elena emerged, wearing a thin, transparent gown over a garter with fishnet nylons and high heels. She walked down the stairs and Miri followed, stopping in front of Vlad.

Vlad sat up when he saw Elena. "Jerzy. You've outdone yourself with this one," he said. He scanned Elena up and down.

"This is Elena," said Jerzy. "Sit. Both of you."

Elena sat on one side of Vlad and Miri on the other.

"I think I would like to go upstairs with you,"

said Vlad. He looked at Miri. "You also."

"Take the penthouse," said Jerzy. "It's all yours."

"You know I would expect nothing less," said Vlad. He stood and said to Elena, "Lead the way." He followed Elena up the stairs. Miri followed. Vlad put his hand between Elena's legs as she slowly climbed.

* *

Vlad sauntered down the stairway zipping up the jacket of his track suit after finishing with Elena and Miri. Jerzy sat at the table, a good portion of the Absolut gone, staring into space.

Vlad sat in the chair opposite Jerzy. "You taught them well," said Vlad. "The other, although older…." His voice trailed off. "I want them both."

"Elena is a big money maker," he said, reconciling to the fact that Elena would soon be gone. "My best. I keep her in reserve, like a fine whiskey. Very tame with her, let's say, treatments. She can get fiery, though, without. She is dependent, only mildly. Give her what she needs and she settles down." Jerzy sat back. "Miri will do whatever a client wants. Anything, anytime, drugs or no drugs."

"Let's talk business," said Vlad. "Name a price and we go from there."

"Thirty five thousand. Deutschmarks," said Jerzy.

"That's a lot, my old friend," said Vlad, his eyes hardening. "Friends do not gouge friends on price."

"No less than twenty five. Deutschmarks," said Jerzy.

Vlad nodded. "Ten thousand. American dollars. For both," he said.

Jerzy sat up. "I do not want to let Elena go. Not for that," he said.

"I can see why," said Vlad. "Where did you find her?"

"Let's just say she found her way to me," said Jerzy, taking a drink of vodka.

Vlad looked coolly at Jerzy. "Fifteen. Fifteen thousand is more than generous, don't you agree?"

"Euros," said Jerzy.

"Dollars," said Vlad.

Jerzy looked at the pocket where Vlad put the phone.

"Deal."

Vlad smiled. "Good. I will be back tomorrow."

CHAPTER 16

Dogfight

Cletus B. Lincoln parked the rusty Jeep Cherokee four houses down the block. Great vehicle for this neighborhood- rugged, could four-wheel through just about anything or anybody. Lincoln just shook his head at the pimp machines, two parked ahead, near the house. Big tittie hood ornaments, lake pipes, gangsta walls, spin wheels and shag interiors. Dumb asses. The DPD loved these rides, easy to track and place at a crime scene.

He looked in the rear view mirror before getting out of the Jeep. He tried to look away from his nose but couldn't help it, almost flattened and pushed to one side. Never healed right.

...Lincoln couldn't stand the sight of the kid. Dirty, little motherfucker. Funky smelling. It was a game, harassing him. Take shit away from him, cookies, chips, pop, whatever. Didn't matter, just as long as he had something worth taking. The kid just stood there and took

it, not saying anything, not crying. Lincoln laughing with his friends, making faces and eating or drinking what they took. Kid never had any money. How old was he? Seven, eight? His mama didn't say shit either. Always with some new dude, every time Lincoln would see her...

Lincoln remembered walking to the party store with his mother, seeing the punk's mama working the corner, laughing and cackling with a couple of dudes. Lincoln's mother grabbed his sleeve and strode by with her nose literally in the air.

One day, in front of a couple of girls Lincoln cornered him and tried pulling the kid's pants down. The girls giggled while Lincoln bobbed and weaved, grabbing at the kid's baggy jeans. He got the jeans halfway down, the girls squealing, when the kid stood firm and landed a roundhouse on Lincoln's left ear. Lincoln still remembered the impact, the popping sound as the air compressed in his ear canal, the bright flash, and shock. He remembered dropping to the ground. The kid straddled him and pummeled away at his face, finally punching him square in the bridge of the nose. Lincoln held his hands over his face, feeling his nose swell to twice its normal size. The girls ran away. The little punk got up, didn't say anything, pulled up his jeans and walked away. Lincoln and his mother moved out at the end of the month. Lincoln never saw him again.

...Learned something from it, though. Don't be direct. Back door it. If you want to fuck someone over, do it indirectly, from behind. Never hit them head on...

Lincoln walked down the sidewalk then turned left toward a neglected asbestos shingle bungalow. He walked up the broken concrete driveway into the dirt back yard, looking at some dog pens in the garage. Lincoln passed three dog pens made from two by fours and chain link fence. The corner fence was chewed away on the third pen, leaving a trace of blood and fur. He wished he knew what dog lived in that pen. He would bet on him.

He walked up the wooden porch and knocked on the steel barred door. The door opened. Dude looked like one of Alanzo's homies, which was good. Lincoln paid his sixty five dollar entrance fee, stepped in and looked around.

Alanzo turned the corner from the hall and stopped when he saw Lincoln.

"Man, you got some balls showing up here," said Alanzo, flashing his diamond studded front teeth.

"Sup, dog. Man's got a right to make a wager," said Lincoln.

Alanzo nodded. "That's true, homes."

Lincoln looked beyond Alazo into the front room. Two treadmills, thick ropes, cattle prod, rape stand, syringes on an end table. They walked through the threadbare kitchen and down the stairs where dudes stood around a blood stained fighting pen. The smell- sweat, dog shit, excitement and fear hit Lincoln and he stopped momentarily.

Alanzo looked at him. "Like that smell?" Alanzo breathed in deeply. "Man, that's power."

Lincoln looked at the ring.

"This ain't no street show," said Alanzo. "Cajun Rules. Classy."

The fighting pit was square, the sides two feet high and the scratch line twelve feet apart, right according to Cajun Rules. The referee was searching the handlers, before they washed each other's dogs. Two stocky American pit bulls. Lincoln heard of both of them. Little Joe Louis, a Grand Champion, knew how to win but was aging and got torn up the last two shows. The challenger, Ripper, was young, had game and hadn't lost a show yet. The referee nodded and each of the handlers scrubbed down the other's dog and toweled them off. Alanzo and Lincoln watched carefully.

"Was at one gang show," said Alanzo. "Real ghetto shit. Didn't wash the dogs. No rules. One was slicked down with three-in-one oil, rubbed in so you couldn't see it, laced with rat poison. Fucked up the other dog big time. Had to be put down." He looked at Lincoln. "Handler and owner got capped."

"Happens every day," said Lincoln. He looked at Alanzo. "Wanted to let you know. Our little project. Our friend is making it happen. As we speak."

"Alright," said Alanzo. "I'm ready when y'all are."

"He'll be back next week," said Lincoln. "A little after that we should be good to go."

"That's what I like to hear," said Alanzo.

The referee told the handlers to get in their corners. The handlers held their dogs facing away from each other. The referee then said, "Face your dogs."

The handlers turned and stood over the dogs, showing only their heads and shoulders. Little Joe Louis's handler felt the dog tighten. Reminded him of a cobra, ready to strike.

"Let go," said the referee.

Both dogs roared toward the scratch line, legs like springs. Little Joe leapt and went for Ripper's throat. Ripper dodged but Little Joe caught the base of Ripper's ear just above the left eye and bit through. Ripper yelped, flipped over and clamped on Little Joe's left inner hind leg. He sunk in his teeth and shook hard. Little Joe howled and blood spurted from his leg.

"C'mon, motherfucker," yelled Alanzo.

Little Joe kicked, squirmed and snapped at Ripper. He caught Ripper in his underbelly and broke skin. Ripper cried and Little Joe broke free. Little Joe Louis did what he was famous for. In a blur his jaws clamped on Ripper's throat. Ripper gasped for air and went down, kicking and scratching. Ripper snapped his jaws twice then collapsed.

The referee motioned to the handlers. Little Joe's handler barked a couple of commands but the dog wouldn't let go. Ripper lay on the pit floor, near the scratch line.

"That's my motherfuckin' dog," said Alanzo, laughing.

Lincoln put two grand on Ripper. He shook his head. "I should hand the bitch his balls who told me to bet on that lame ass mutt."

The referee told Little Joe's handler to get a break stick. The handler rushed to his corner and picked up a wooden axe handle. He worked it in Little Joe's mouth and after three minutes pried Little Joe's jaws open, releasing Ripper. Ripper, barely conscious and bleeding, lay on the pit floor.

"No big whoop," said Alanzo, who stood to collect fifteen thousand dollars from the five he bet. The payout started and Alanzo took his cash.

Lincoln thought of what he could have done with the extra two grand he just lost. "You're right," he said to Alanzo. "Ain't nothin' compared to what's comin' in."

They turned and walked toward the stairs. Little Joe Louis was outside of the pit, being cleaned up by his handler and owner. Ripper lay on the pit floor, his handler standing above him with a shovel. No doubt he had to put Ripper down.

Lincoln and Alanzo turned and walked toward the stairs, never noticing the short, jet black dude in the gray hoodie. Clarence Russell turned and watched them climb the stairs, after catching bits of conversation, wondered what was going down. He also remembered with perfect clarity, just like it was this morning, how it felt to flatten Lincoln's face.

CHAPTER 17

Elena Leaves Albania

Elena sat on the bed, chilled, goose bumps forming on her arms and legs. She felt empty and dizzy, spinning, like she was falling off a cliff. The needle. Feeling like this, it wasn't so terrifying. She shifted position. It still hurt to sit in one spot for very long.

Last night's final client was bizarre, a well dressed, well placed government official. His bodyguard stood outside the door. Jerzy arranged for Miri and Elena to perform for him. He sat naked in the armchair and directed them. Miri took the lead, telling Elena to smile and act like she was getting off. Any complaints and Jerzy would punish them. Severely. Miri went to work and Elena put herself somewhere else. The client finished himself, then left.

Miri sat at the vanity brushing her hair. Elena shivered. When was her last hit? Twelve, fourteen hours ago? A wave of nausea and diarrhea hit her. She rushed to the toilet, just making it into the bathroom. She crawled to the bowl, naked and vomiting, fouling the floor. She hung over the bowl, shaking.

"I can't do this. I can't stand it anymore. I want my daughter or I want to die." She stared weeping.

Miri walked in and stood over her, then leaned down and helped her to her feet.

"Come," she said. "Let's clean you up." She cleaned the floor and flushed the toilet. She started drawing a bath in the small porcelain tub. Elena shook and sobbed. The tub filled with warm water and Miri helped her in.

"Don't cry," said Miri. "Steel yourself. Put yourself somewhere pleasant in your mind."

Elena felt relief in the warm water. She stared at the dripping faucet.

"Is that what you do?" she said. Since last night she had trouble looking Miri in the eyes.

Miri nodded.

"Why have you stayed here?" said Elena.

The sensation of falling returned. Elena gripped the side of the tub. Miri watched Elena tense up in the tub. Jerzy was giving her too much junk and waiting too long between hits. Miri saw it with other girls, coming down hard. Elena seems to be handling it better than some, worse than others. Elena was strong, but so were others...for a while. The ones that were too dependent were used up until they died.

"How can I leave?" said Miri. "How can any of us leave? No one cares about us. We are cows, to be milked until dry and left to die when younger ones come." She looked down at Elena. "You are young now, but not so much. One year here will age you by five."

Elena sat up, the dizziness and nausea fading.

Even in the warm water her muscles ached and cramped.

"Can't we escape?" she said.

"To where? The mountains?" said Miri. "The army is worse than the ones that come here. Trust me."

"Have you ever tried?"

Miri paused. "Yes," she said. "Four years ago."

"What happened?"

Miri's eyes went distant. "I made it as far as the next village. It was winter. January. I almost froze to death." Miri lit a cigarette, took a drag and exhaled. "I was picked up by a farmer. He took one look at me and brought me right back to Jerzy." Miri tapped the ash over the sink. "Jerzy pays the locals well. For watching out for him, and for favors. Bringing me back was a favor."

Miri turned and opened her robe, exposing her left side. Four small circular scars were under her ribs. "No doubt you've wondered about these. He beat me and burned me with a cigarette. You've seen the scars on my back. He said if I tried to escape again he would kill me. As an example, no matter how much money I brought in."

Miri held up her left hand. "Jerzy left me with a special client. A small man, dark. Like a weasel. He had a special request which Jerzy did not honor until I tried to escape."

Elena looked at the stump of Miri's missing little finger. Jerzy tied me down and left. The little man got undressed and was excited. He had a small surgical saw, like a butcher's knife with teeth." Miri put her hand in her lap. "He sawed off my finger, slowly. I passed out. Jerzy said the client kept it as a souvenir."

Elena slid back into the water and stared at the ceiling.

Miri looked down. "After I recovered, I would service at least twenty men a day. One right after another, for almost a month. Do anything they wanted to do, and do it with a smile." She looked at Elena, her dark hair floating around her head. "Do not put yourself in that position. Please."

Elena looked at her. "I will kill myself."

"That's what you say," said Miri. "But what about your daughter? Leave her an orphan?"

"She is like an orphan now," said Elena. She started to cry.

"No man?" said Miri.

"Killed. By a gang of so-called rebels. He did nothing to them." Elena started shaking.

"Hold on," said Miri. She left the bathroom and walked to the vanity. She opened a drawer and pulled out a brown bottle of painkillers, took two out and walked back into the bathroom. She handed them to Elena. "Here," she said. "Take them."

Elena took the pills, put them in her mouth, raised her head back and swallowed them. They felt dry and abrasive in her throat.

"Listen to me," said Miri. "Live for your daughter. Take the pills. Cooperate with Jerzy. Be nice and he might stop shooting you up. Take the pills only when you absolutely need to. Fight it."

Elena slid back into the tub. Relief poured over her like warm rain.

* *

Miri helped Elena out of the tub and used a clean white towel to dry her. Elena put on a robe and sat on the bed, buzzed from the painkillers. Not the same floating high as heroin, but it was pleasant and even.

Jerzy burst into the room.

"Pack your things," he said. "Both of you."

"Why?" said Miri.

"You're leaving. With Vlad."

Elena looked up. "Where are we going?"

"Don't complain," said Jerzy. "Vlad is taking you to America."

"America?" cried Elena.

"Shut up and pack your things."

Miri started gathering clothes and makeup. Elena sat on the bed with her head in her hands.

"Consider yourself lucky," said Jerzy. "But make no mistake. Cross Vlad and he will kill you as easy as killing a cockroach. You are no more than an investment to him." He pulled Elena's head up by her chin. "And you better pay off."

CHAPTER 18

Zippy Shows Paulie the Ropes

Eddie sat in his wheelchair at the table, cup of coffee in his hand, pleased that his fence said no problem on converting three hundred k to diamonds. He could have them by Wednesday, straight from New York if Eddie gave him the cash, plus a service fee. He took a sip of coffee and watched Zippy and Paulie.

"What do you know about cars?" asked Zippy.

"I like fast ones," said Paulie, chewing gum.

"First thing you gotta know is how to take 'em apart and put 'em together," said Zippy.

"That so," said Paulie.

"Damn right. That's why the best guys come from repair shops and assembly lines. Dudes either built, seen or fixed most everything," said Zippy.

"I wouldn't know, man," said Paulie.

Zippy looked at him, cigarette behind his slick black hair, expensive t-shirt, designer jeans, expensive shoes. Not exactly the type of clothes to be busting down cars.

Eddie, paging through a copy of Hustler, kept an eye on them.

"First thing you gotta know about boosting cars, especially expensive ones, is disabling the telematics unit," he said.

"The what?" asked Paulie.

The telematics unit. Automatically calls for help if the car crashes. Tracks position from GPS," said Zippy. "Satellites. Man. Up in space. Knows where you're at. Some of the units automatically call the cops," he said. "Car gets boosted, goes out of a zone, signal sent to the owner and the cops. They can track you all the way, man, even kill the engine."

"I didn't know that," said Paulie.

"Now you do," said Zippy. There's other systems too. Pull a couple of fuses, cut a couple of wires, no problem. The thing's dead and no one has a clue. I'll show you how to disable them. First," said Zippy, "you need to get dirty, start small."

Zippy put his hands in his back pocket. "I'll show you how to boost rims," he said. "Easy and good money." They walked over to a beater Ford Taurus that Zippy was working on. He motioned toward a hydraulic jack. "Grab that jack and bring it over."

"Me?" said Paulie.

"No, Eddie," said Zippy. "Yeah, you."

Paulie frowned and walked slowly over to the jack, grabbed it by the handle and brought it over.

"Man, you got to hustle," said Zippy. "Like a NASCAR dude."

Paulie dropped the jack handle and it bounced, clanking on the floor.

"I thought I was gonna see some action. Go

on a real boost. This is a shit job," he said.

"You don't send a new soldier into a war without training, do you?" said Zippy. "He'd get killed right away. And this is a war. It only looks easy."

"I can handle it," said Paulie. "No problem."

"Let me ask you this," said Zippy. "Have you ever changed a tire?"

"Couple of times."

Eddie put the magazine down and called them over.

Eddie looked at Paulie and said, "Your uncle and I go way, way back. I don't know what he told you."

"He said you were in Viet Nam together."

"That's right," said Eddie. "Carried me out when I got shot. I owe him for that." Eddie adjusted himself in the chair and said, "Why did he really send you here?"

Paulie shrugged. "You know. To learn the business."

Eddie looked at him. "You don't know the first thing about cars."

"That's why I'm here. To learn."

Eddie sat back. "You know," he said. "Nobody gets into this business without having cars in their blood. At least I don't know anybody. It hurts me that your uncle doesn't trust me."

"He trusts you," said Paulie.

"If he did, you wouldn't be here." Eddie thought for a moment. "You want to go on a boost?"

"Sure do," said Paulie.

"He ain't ready," said Zippy.

"I'm ready," said Paulie. "I'm fuckin' ready right now."

"No you aren't," said Zippy.

Eddie held up his hand. "Hold it. Both of you." He looked at Zippy. "Cool it for a minute."

"I'm tellin' you, he ain't ready," said Zippy.

Eddie rolled out from behind the table and looked at Paulie. "Make a deal with you," said Eddie. "Tell me why you're here and you go on a boost. Tomorrow."

"To learn how to steal cars. Learn the business," said Paulie.

Eddie stared at him for a moment, then shook his head. "Forget it. Forget I said anything." He looked at Zippy. "You done with him for today?"

"Wait a minute," said Paulie.

"Never mind, kid," said Eddie. "Forget about it."

Paulie hesitated, and then said, "Tomorrow?"

"Just answer the question and you're good to go."

Paulie put his hands in his back pockets, looked at the floor and said, "To watch you."

"Why?" said Eddie.

"To see if you got something going with some Albanian guy."

Eddie looked at him a long time, and then rolled back behind the table.

"Why does he think that?" he said.

"He thinks you're playing him. He don't like it."

"What did he want you to do?" said Eddie.

Paulie shrugged. "See if the guy ever showed up here. See if you ever talked about him. About deals."

Eddie shook his head. "Well, you can let Vinnie know that I don't know anything about any Albanian. Pure and simple." He looked at Zippy. "Take him with you tomorrow, on that thing we talked about."

"No offense," said Zippy. "But he can't even change a tire let alone handle a boost."

"I can handle it," said Paulie.

"This one is hit or miss," said Eddie. "A long shot." He looked at Zippy. "Don't take any unnecessary chances. Walk if you have to."

"Goes without saying," said Zippy.

"Go or no go, it's your call and your call alone," said Eddie. He looked at Paulie. "Two things. First, you do everything, and I mean everything Zippy tells you to do. To the tee. Got it?"

"Got it," said Paulie.

"And second, out little conversation here doesn't get back to Vinnie."

"Got that too," said Paulie.

* *

Zippy told Paulie to wear a shirt and tie. A clip on, to look as legit as possible and not get it hung up on anything. They sat in a stolen Impala across from the Book Cadillac hotel. The hauler was parked near the main entrance. One BMW was already loaded. The driver walked down one of the ramps after securing it with the straps and frame chains.

"This is where it pays to keep up on what's going on around town," said Zippy. "Happens a few times a year, not only during the auto show. Manufacturers bring in their rides to show off and shuttle execs around." Zippy wiped the steering wheel with a moist towelette and handed one to Paulie. "If it happens, open up the door with this. Wipe it down. Outside handle too. No fingerprints." Zippy put the towelette on the console. "Commercial real estate convention this week. People in from all over the country. Draws top end car makers like flies."

The driver was eyeballing the cab when the valet pulled up in a 325i. The valet got out and left it running. The hauler driver got in, drove it up the ramp and secured it. The valet turned and walked away. The hauler driver hopped off the rig and looked at his watch.

"This is it," said Zippy. "Get out and wipe down. Put on your sunglasses and follow me."

They got out of the Impala and left the keys. They quickly wiped down the door handles and dropped the towelettes. Zippy glanced at Paulie. Cocky as he was, he pulled that off like a pro.

Zippy had timed how long it took for the valet to bring the cars. Nine minutes. Just enough time to circle the entire block. They crossed Washington in front of the hauler, turned left and walked toward State Street.

"We can make it around in six or seven minutes," said Zippy. "That'll give us two minutes to make a move. If it's clear, I'll drive. You ride shotgun."

"Okay, man," said Paulie, literally bouncing as he walked. "This is too fucking cool."

"Calm down," said Zippy. He noticed the handle of a pistol near the left side under Paulie's belt.

"Did I tell you to bring a piece?" said Zippy. "Did I? You dumb fuck. Don't ever bring a piece unless I tell you to. I don't even have one."

"Just a little insurance," said Paulie.

"You do not, I repeat, do not, bring a piece on a boost like this."

They turned the corner onto State Street. About midway Zippy looked at his watch. Five minutes. "Breathe deep," he said. "That's the first thing you gotta learn. Be cool, and be aware. Look around without looking around. Notice everything."

"Okay, man, okay," said Paulie, breathing in deeply. They turned the corner onto Griswold.

Zippy looked at his watch. Four minutes. "Let's pick it up a little."

They picked up their pace and a minute later turned the corner onto Michigan Avenue. As they passed the 24Grille the valet whizzed by in a 760Li. Zippy looked at his watch. He was off by a minute. "Let's move," he said.

They turned onto Washington and saw the valet step out of the BMW, leaving the door open and the car running. Instead of getting in the BMW, the hauler driver walked back to the cab, opened the door, stepped up and leaned in.

"Now," said Zippy. "Go."

They sprinted toward the BMW. Zippy hopped in the driver's seat and Paulie slid in the other side. Zippy slammed it in reverse then put it in drive and squealed around the hauler. The hauler driver stepped out of the cab holding a cell phone. He watched the BMW disappear down Washington.

CHAPTER 19

Amateur Night

"We could do something to the air conditioning," said Washington. "Or mess with the utilities to get inside."

Peabody shook her head. "No way. They'd read it like a book. If anything went south, air conditioner, lights, plumbing, name it, you can bet an Albanian contractor will be on the job. A trusted one."

"So what do we do? Let the court order go to waste just because we can't execute?"

Peabody thought for a moment and said, "amateur night."

* *

Washington picked up Peabody in the parking lot adjacent to the Bunker. He almost didn't recognize her. Her bright blond hair was teased out and sprayed, stripper style. She wore loads of makeup, reddish cheeks, dark blue eye shadow and thick black mascara. She had on a short rabbit fur coat stopping above her bare knees, and wore high platform shoes.

Washington pulled beside her, reached over and opened the door. Peabody got in, her fur coat riding up her thighs.

"Ready for this?" she said.

"I'm speechless," said Washington. "I'd take you for a stripper any day."

"Thank you," said Peabody. "That's the point."

They drove along Eight Mile towards the Tiger's Den.

"It's pretty much the same everywhere, strip joints," said Peabody. "Amateur night is usually slow. Some regulars don't show up, cause a lot of the steady dancers bust their butts on weekends and have Monday or Tuesday night off. A lot are turning tricks."

Washington breathed in Peabody's perfume, smelled like roses and musk. She smelled good. Really good. "How come you know so much about strip clubs?"

"Worked in one when I was in law school. Made a ton of money."

Washington nodded.

"Not in Ithaca, though," said Peabody. "Up in Syracuse. On weekends, sometimes on weeknights. I could make more in a couple of nights than any other part time job at the time. Plus, I didn't have to think. Get the basic pole moves down and just go on autopilot." She looked at Washington. "My stripper name was Penny."

"No problem taking your clothes off?"

"No big deal," said Peabody. "First time was a little shaky, but after that, no problem. Spent my time thinking about contracts and torts."

"What about tonight?"

"I'll take 'em off if I have to," said Peabody. "I want that place bugged."

Washington watched the road.

"We know the layout," said Peabody. "We'll order drinks, settle in, and you'll go to the men's room, right next to the office. Dragovic is a continent away so all we have to worry about is the staff. And the bouncer."

"Sounds pretty iffy to me," said Washington.

"If you have a shot at the office, take it. Put it under a desk or a chair if you can. If you can't get near the office, put it in the john. Maybe we can pick something up there."

Peabody looked out the window, seeing the darkened iron-gated storefronts pass by. "It's a long shot, but you never know. We might get lucky." She pulled the sun visor down and popped open the mirror, checking her makeup.

Washington pulled into the Tiger's Den parking lot.

"Ready for this?" said Peabody.

Washington nodded. They got out and walked to the entrance, under the buzzing neon sign. Washington held the door open for Peabody. She stepped through and scanned the interior. Three couples sat at small tables near the stage. One of the real strippers was onstage, Kool and the Gang thumping in the background. Four guys sat at the bar, along with a little guy in a wheelchair. Two regular strippers talked to him. The bouncer was talking to the bartender.

The couples near the stage watched the stripper, turning upside down on the pole, her dyed-red hair spinning. Peabody looked at the couples. She'd seen it before and was still surprised how many guys got off watching their girlfriends or wives dance naked.

Peabody and Washington sat at a table equal distance from the stage and the hall leading to the restrooms. The only barmaid working walked over, laid down a couple of cocktail napkins and said with an accent, "Welcome to the Tiger's Den. There's a two drink minimum."

Washington shrugged and looked at Peabody. "What'll you have?"

"Gin and tonic," said Peabody. "With lime."

"I'll have a PBR," said Washington.

The barmaid turned and walked toward the bar. Peabody looked at Washington. "PBR?"

"Hey. I've been drinking that long before it became hip."

The regular stripper ran off the stage. The lights started flashing and the bouncer walked on the stage and said in a thick accent, "welcome to amateur time." He looked at the couples. "Who go first?"

A woman at the middle table raised her hand and stood. The lights started flashing and the woman strolled onto the stage, overweight and wearing a bikini. Washington looked at her stomach folding over the top of her thong. She turned and wiggled her butt, rumpled with cellulite. She smiled, shook her hips, held her arm straight and pointed at her husband. Led Zeppelin blasted in the background. Washington looked away. The barmaid came with the drinks and Washington paid her.

The woman on stage gyrated around the pole, out of time with the music. She popped out of her top, pulled it off and tossed at her husband who whooped and clapped. He laughed and looked around at the other tables.

"Jesus," said Washington.

Peabody leaned over. "They're called BBWs. Big Breasted Women. Some guys love 'em."

The woman pranced on stage. Peabody watched for a moment then subtly scanned the room. The bouncer patted one of the guys at the bar on the back then walked down the hall past the restrooms and toward the office.

Peabody nudged Washington. "The bouncer. Looks like he's headed toward the office. Give it a shot."

Washington got up and walked toward the hall. Peabody watched the woman on stage and bopped her head to the music.

Washington saw the bouncer inside the office as he opened the door to the men's room. The office was sparse- a wooden desk, leather swivel chair, a couple of filing cabinets and a sofa with a baseball bat leaning against it. The bouncer's cell phone rang and he pulled it from his pocket.

Washington ducked into the men's room and waited, listening by the door. He heard the bouncer talking, but not clearly. He heard enough to realize the bouncer wasn't speaking English. The conversation stopped and a moment later the men's room door opened.

Washington rushed to the sink and turned on the faucet. The bouncer gave him a look that he knew well, *the you're the wrong color, what are you doing here stare*. The bouncer walked into the stall and Washington heard the toilet seat bounce off the rim of the bowl. The bouncer sat and let loose. Washington quickly dried his hands and walked out of the men's room. He looked around and went in the office, pulling the small bug from his pants pocket. He removed the waxy paper from the adhesive pad and placed the bug underneath the desktop overhang, feeling it set securely to the surface. He tried to wiggle it, but the bug held firm. Washington walked out of the office and heard clapping and yelling coming from the tables around the stage.

He turned the corner and saw Peabody stepping off the stage, putting her thin silky top on. The guys at the bar stood and clapped. So did the little guy in the wheelchair, who put two fingers to his mouth and whistled.

Peabody put her fur coat on and sat down, sweating from the hot stage lights. A man from the next table whispered something to his wife, got up and walked over to Peabody.

"Great show," he said. Peabody looked up at him. "My wife and I were wondering maybe you could come over and join us? You and your friend? Have a drink?"

Washington arrived at the table, sat down and looked at the man.

"Thanks," said Peabody. "But we really have to go. Maybe some other time."

"Sure you can't stay?" The guy glanced back at his wife and shook his head.

Peabody nodded. "Can't do it. Sounds tempting, though," she said. "Sorry."

"Okay," he said. "Could have partied together." He walked back to his wife, shrugged and sat down.

"We all good?" said Peabody.

"Think so."

Two dudes at the bar stared at Washington, the only black guy in the place. Black guy with a hot white blond. The two guys talked, looked at Washington then started talking again. The bouncer joined them, one of the guys said something, and then the bouncer stared.

"I think it's time to go," said Washington.

"I'm ready when you are," said Peabody. "Just make it look good."

Washington put his arm around Peabody. They walked out the front entrance and through the parking lot and got in the car. Washington started it and they pulled out of the lot onto Eight Mile. The two guys who sat at the bar burst through the entrance and watched Washington and Peabody drive away. They looked at each other. One of them said, "Lucky son of a bitch."

CHAPTER 20

Chris Makes a Pickup

Chris lay back on the double bed watching television, his head propped up by two pillows. His cell phone and pager sat within reach on the small nightstand. He twisted a cap off a bottle of beer. Drinking while on call was forbidden, but he never once got a call on Wednesday night.

He flipped through the channels with the remote when his phone rang. Chris put down the remote and looked at the incoming number. Florida area code, Miami. He pressed the green answer button.

"Hello?"

"Is this Chris?"

"Yes."

"Hi Chris. Adam Wilkins here."

"Adam, how are you man," said Chris. "I've been meaning to call you."

"I haven't heard from you in awhile."

"How's the boat?" said Chris.

"That's what I wanted to talk to you about."

"What's up?"

"Look, Chris. I'm not a man to go back on an agreement, more of an understanding, really. I got an offer. A good one."

Chris felt like he was just punched in the stomach.

"How much?" said Chris.

"I don't want to say, but it beats yours. Substantially."

Chris held the phone to his ear, trying to think of something to say.

"The interested party has cash. All they want is a quick survey. If the boat checks out, which it will, they want immediate possession."

"I thought we had a deal," said Chris.

"We had an understanding. Maybe less than that. How can I commit to the extra time you want when I have a better offer and can close in a week?"

"What if I send you some cash? In good faith," said Chris.

"What good would that do? There's no guarantee you could come up with the rest."

"I'll come up with it," said Chris. "No worries here."

Chris sat down on the bed and looked around for a cigarette. "How about this," he said. "Give me three weeks, maybe a little more. Get the boat surveyed. I didn't care about that 'cause I trust you and know you take good care of it. Like I will."

Not seeing his pack of cigarettes, Chris picked up a long butt from an ashtray. "It'll take a week or so to get it surveyed and the report back, right? And it'll take the buyer some time to look it over. That's probably close to two weeks there." Chris lit the butt and inhaled. "What's two, maybe three more weeks gonna do?"

Silence on the other end.

"You know how bad I want the boat, and I'll take care of it," said Chris. "Not just the boat, but the charter. Keep it going." He looked down at the cigarette's orange tip. "That's gotta mean something."

"All right. Three weeks. At most. Tell you the truth, I'd rather sell it to you, but an offer's an offer."

Chris exhaled.

"Thank you."

* *

Chris butted the cigarette in the ashtray and realized he was out. He picked up the beer and took a swig. His pager beeped. He set the beer down, picked up the pager and looked at the number. This wasn't a code but a call in number. Dispatch. Chris pressed a button on the pager, picked up his cell phone and dialed the number. After a couple of rings a female voice answered on the other end.

"Number seven here. Wolfe," said Chris. "Just got a page to call in. What's up?"

"Hold on," said the dispatcher. After a moment she said, "Airport run. Metro."

"I'm on call for the RenCen tonight," said Chris.

"I know, but this was called in special. The client specifically asked for you."

"What time?" said Chris.

"Nine thirty. You better move."

Chris looked at his watch. Eight forty three. Should be enough time to hop on 94, shoot through Detroit and Dearborn then across Romulus to the airport.

"What terminal? Who am I looking for?"

"International. Party's name is Dragovic."

"On my way," said Chris.

* *

No one noticed the unmarked Impala with the lightly tinted windows standing near the Air France check-in at the International Terminal except the airport cop stationed outside. He studied the Impala and didn't like two things. One, he didn't like the tinted windows, and two, it was standing there way too long.

Washington noticed him first. "Get your badge out," he said to Peabody. "Maybe we can call him off."

Peabody watched the cop cross the service drive and walk towards them. "Got it," she said, reaching for her badge.

The cop slowed as he neared the car, peering through the tinted windows, seeing a black male and a white female in the passenger's seat. He put his hand over his service weapon and walked to the driver's side.

Washington rolled down the window. Peabody held her badge out.

"Ann Peabody, DEA," she said. The cop examined the badge.

"Freeman Washington, DPD auto." Washington flashed his.

"Right now, you're interfering with an undercover investigation," said Peabody.

"I had to check you out," said the cop.

"Not a problem," said Peabody. "Help us out. Just step away and keep our line of sight clear."

"Sure thing," said the cop.

"Now, please," said Peabody. Washington was impressed with Peabody's authoritative tone.

The cop turned an about face and walked back across the service drive. Washington rolled up the window and Peabody fiddled with the digital camera with a large zoom lens. The vehicle's lightly tinted windows did not block a lot of visible light from entering, just heat. Peabody raised the camera, focused on the entrance then put the camera in her lap.

"Now we wait," she said.

* *

Vlad Dragovic emerged from the terminal walking between two women, one of them strikingly beautiful.

"Hey," said Peabody. "There he is. With two women." She raised the camera and clicked off some shots. Vlad carried a big duffel bag over his shoulder and the women each toted small suitcases on casters.

Chris saw Vlad and the women at the pickup area in front of the terminal. Vlad stood out, a head taller than most people, wearing an ivory track suit with blue stripes down the side and a matching baseball cap. Chris focused on Elena. My God, where did she come from? Wearing tight sweats, hair pulled back in a ponytail, obvious travel clothes. Dark hair, big eyes, innocent looking yet incredibly sexy. Only a few women ever made him feel this way on first sight. That was a long time ago and he'd forgotten the weak, warm, almost sad feeling.

The other woman, attractive but older smoked a cigarette. Chris pulled up in front of them. Vlad looked in and smiled. Chris popped open the trunk, got out and went for the bags.

"My favorite taxi driver," said Vlad.

Chris smiled. "How many times do I have to say it. This is a limo, not a taxi." Chris had a hard time not staring at Elena. He smiled at her and she smiled back, weakly.

This chick was definitely buzzed. He loaded the bags and held the door open for them. Miri got in first, then Vlad and Elena.

"Where to?" said Chris.

"My club," said Vlad. "My new ladies will be attractions there."

"Very nice," said Chris.

Vlad turned to Elena. "This young man will be working for me, soon," he said.

"Maybe you should get to know him."

"That's news to me," said Chris.

Vlad leaned forward. "Why don't you come my club tonight. You and Eddie. We can talk, and maybe you can get to know the girls a little better."

They didn't notice the Impala. Peabody shot rapid frames of Vlad, Elena, Miri and Chris. The limo drove away. Peabody and Washington followed them down I-94 to I-75 northbound then onto Eight Mile. They passed the club in the far left lane and Vlad, Miri and Elena entered the club.

"Court order or no court order, let's bug Dragovic's car," said Peabody.

CHAPTER 21

At the Tiger's Den

Chris watched Elena twirl slowly around the pole. He felt the music thumping in his chest. Besides the girls, that's the one thing he liked about strip clubs- the music. Music was more real, more primal, playing loud with a beautiful naked woman dancing to it.

Eddie and Vlad sat at a table near the stage drinking Absolut, Miri at Eddie's side. Chris sat next to Vlad and took a swig from a bottle of Bud. He made eye contact with Elena. She momentarily broke out of her robotic, faraway gaze and brightened.

A group of men sat near the stage, enthralled by Elena. Chris watched them. Two wore white shirts and ties, young but with beer bellies, waistbands rolling over their belts. Probably had wives and kids at home, steady nine to five jobs and happy to have them. Chris wondered what it would be like to live like that. Stable. Maybe be an engineer or accountant. He figured he would last about two months. Follow a coffee cup around for thirty years? No thanks.

Elena slowly spun around the pole, got on her hands and knees and crawled toward them. She stopped at the edge of the stage, rolled on her back and spread her legs. The two guys wearing ties whooped and high fived each other, dollar bills in their hands. The other guy stood silent and mesmerized. Elena got on her knees and the guys tucked the bills into the side of her g-string. Elena swung her head around, her dark hair rolling like a wave of sex-charged surf.

"Goddamn," said Eddie. "She's a hot one." He looked at Vlad. "I shoulda opened a strip club."

The music stopped and the guys near the stage stood and clapped. Vlad motioned to Elena. She walked off the stage under the watchful eye of the bouncer. She was poised, but somewhat unstable. Chris couldn't tell if she was buzzed or dizzy from the stage gyrations. Vlad pointed to the chair next to Chris and Elena sat down and smiled, blankly.

"You're a good dancer," said Chris, instantly feeling stupid and awkward. Dumb thing to say.

"Thank you," said Elena.

"You speak English well," he said, again feeling dumb. It had been awhile since he sat with a beautiful naked woman. He tried not to stare at her tits.

The music started again and another dancer, young with short black hair started spinning upside down on the pole. Vlad leaned over and said, "Elena, take my friend in the back room. For a private dance."

Elena looked at Vlad, then Chris and said, "come with me." She stood and took Chris's hand.

"Have fun, buddy," said Eddie. He looked at Miri, who was playing with his ear. "Man," he said. "If my junk still worked."

Elena led Chris to one of the lap dance rooms in the rear. "Sit here," she said, leading him to an oversized leather easy chair. Chris sat and Elena straddled him. She put her arms behind her head and let her hair slip through her fingers. She gyrated on Chris's lap, moving up and down, pressing her breasts lightly against his face. She smelled like warm, wet lavender.

"You like?" whispered Elena.

"Yes I do," said Chris. She smiled, then looked away and went back to someplace distant.

* *

Vlad and Eddie moved to the office. Vlad sat behind the desk and Eddie wheeled to the front. He looked at the bat leaning against the couch.

"Our shipment is here," said Vlad. "All we need now is to have someone pick it up."

"Where is it?" said Eddie.

"Somewhere far from here," said Vlad.

"So what's the plan?"

"Your guy," said Vlad, motioning to the room where Elena was working Chris. "The taxi driver."

Vlad sat back, his knee just missing the bug under the desk. "They make an attractive pair, do they not?"

Eddie shrugged his shoulders. "I guess so."

"They will pose as newly married," said Vlad. "On first trip together, how you say, something moon?"

"It's called a honeymoon,'" said Eddie.

"Yes, honeymoon. They go to Canada. Very easy to get documents and cross border. Both ways." Vlad leaned forward. "They will pick up the package and bring it back."

"I dunno, man. I don't know if he'll go for it," said Eddie. "Boosts are one thing, but this…"

Vlad sat back, thinking. "I know what he wants. You told me."

Eddie thought for a moment. "He does have his heart set on that boat."

"This could be a big step toward getting it," said Vlad. "And Elena, she will do whatever I tell her to do, or I will have her daughter killed. Or worse. I will buy and sell her to people with certain tastes. She knows this."

Eddie frowned and wheeled away from the desk.

* *

Vlad pushed a button on his cell phone and a moment later the bouncer walked in.

"Tell the new one with the missing finger to get Eddie's friend. I want to talk to him."

The bouncer nodded then disappeared.

Elena saw Miri walk in the lap dance room. Miri motioned to her. Elena gave Chris a long, soulful look and got off. Jesus, it was a long time since Chris was so turned on by a woman. Even if the look was staged.

"Sorry. Vlad wants to see you," said Miri to Chris.

"Yeah," said Chris. "Perfect timing." He sat for a moment, and then stood up. Miri led him to the office then walked toward the bar.

Chris walked in the office.

"Have a seat," said Vlad. Chris sat in the chair opposite the desk, facing Vlad.

"She is very nice, no?"

"Sure is."

"How would you like to spend more time with her? Go on a little trip?"

"A trip?" said Chris. He looked at Eddie then back at Vlad. "To where?"

"Canada," said Vlad. "A small town."

"Why?" said Chris.

"I need you to pick something up for me and bring it back. A package," said Vlad. "You and Elena can be on," Vlad looked at Eddie, "a honeymoon."

Chris sat back. "What's in the package?"

"Something that is worth a lot to me," said Vlad.

Chris figured it was cash, gold or dope. "I don't know, man. It sounds risky. Very risky."

Vlad nodded. "So are your boosts."

"Not like this," said Chris. "On the boosts, I call the shots."

Vlad nodded. "What about your boat?"

Chris sat up.

"How far away are you from getting it?" said Vlad. "It could be a place where we start negotiating your fee."

"I need another one twenty five," said Chris. "One twenty five and I'm there."

Vlad sat back. "As I told you. My father was a fisherman. I understand. I know the sea. A boat, it becomes part of you. Like a living thing." He looked at Chris. "What does it cost? Total."

"Two fifty," said Chris. "For the boat and take over the business."

"You could make one hundred on this trip," said Vlad.

"I need one twenty five," said Chris.

"Twenty five ain't much," said Eddie. "You could make that on a good boost or two."

"We will see about the twenty five," said Vlad. "Right now, I'm offering you one hundred. And you have the extra benefit of having Elena with you. Do what you want with her."

Chris sat back, looked at Eddie then back at Vlad. If Eddie was here, then he had something to do with this and stood to gain somehow. A hundred for this job and if he cleared twenty five from the Millender boost he'd be free and clear to head down to Florida and clinch the deal. He thought of Elena, still smelling her perfume and wouldn't mind taking a road trip with her.

"When does this happen?" said Chris.

"You can leave tomorrow. I have all the papers ready."

Chris sat for a moment. "I'll do it."

Vlad nodded and stood. "We must shake hands." He held out his hand, and Chris shook it. "It is very important."

* *

Peabody and Washington sat in the white work van, parked a few houses down the side street next to the Tiger's Den and had a clear view of the parking lot. She saw Washington place the GPS transponder under the black CTS's gas tank. She lit it up and it tracked perfectly. Washington hurried back to the van.

"Good job," said Peabody.

"Did you get anything?" said Washington.

Peabody nodded. "Some," she said. "A lot of background noise. Static. It was definitely Dragovic. I can tell by the accent. "Don't know who he was talking to."

Washington nodded.

"It looks like someone is going on a road trip." She pulled a video camera from a black canvas case. "We're going to tape everyone that comes out of there until it's empty."

* *

Vlad left alone at 2:15AM. At 2:45AM the bouncer opened the door. Eddie rolled out followed by Chris. Eddie used the loading lift on the van and got in the driver's seat. Chris sat in the passenger's side.

"Hey," said Peabody. "That looks like the limo driver that picked up Dragovic."

"That it does," said Washington.

CHAPTER 22

Rada and Sanja

Rada sat by the fire in the red velour chair in the parlor, glaring at Sanja. Sanja was playing with Trina and the new doll Sami brought her. She stood the dolls up facing each other, like they were talking. Sanja let the new doll go and focused on Trina, fixing her hair with a tiny toy brush.

"Give me that," said Rada, reaching down and grabbing Trina.

"No," said Sanja, not letting go.

"I said give me that," said Rada, pulling the doll from Sanja's little hands. "This doll is no good. Play with the other one." Rada took Trina and threw her in the fireplace. The doll's thin clothes instantly caught fire, then her hair.

"No," cried Sanja. She got up and ran toward the fireplace. Rada snatched her by the collar of her sweater and dragged her through the parlor.

"I told you not to play with that doll," she said. "How many times?" She forced Sanja through the dining area, kitchen and out the rear door.

"I want Momma," cried Sanja.

"She is gone. She isn't coming back," said Rada. She dragged Sanja toward a wooden shed that stood near the rear of the cottage, by the tree

142

line. "All you have is me now," said Rada. "And you need to learn to be good."

Rada stopped in front of the shed and twisted the metal clasp. Sanja collapsed on the ground, crying.

"Do you know why your mother will not be back? Do you?" Rada leaned down and hovered over Sanja's face. "She doesn't love you any more."

Sanja buried her face in her hands and sobbed.

"Get in," said Rada, picking up Sanja and forcing her into the shed. "And if you tell Papa I put you in here I will make you walk in the fields." Rada shut the shed door and twisted the metal clasp.

Sanja sat on the floor, unable to see, and crawled on the damp, hard packed dirt floor to a corner. She felt the wall, seeing thin bands of bright light through the wall's wooden slats. She sat in a corner diagonal to the door, her chin to her knees and her face in her hands.

Two hours later Rada emerged from the cottage and walked toward the shed. She stopped when she heard Sami's Mercedes rumble up the gravel road. She turned and waited for Sami to stop. He got out of the Mercedes and hugged Rada.

"Where is Milos?" he said.

"In the village. He will be back later this evening."

Sami looked around. "And where is Sanja?"

Rada pointed to the shed. "She's been bad. So much like her mother."

Sami looked at the shed.

"Get her out of there," he said. "Take care of her."

"She's a nuisance," said Rada. "Defiant."

"She may not be a problem much longer," said Sami.

"How's that?"

Sami lowered his voice. "First, Elena is gone. Forever. Jerzy had to sell her."

"So?" said Rada. "I thought you and Jerzy no longer talk."

"Business is business," said Sami. "I just thought you would like to know." He stepped closer. "Jerzy has a new proposition. He is lining up some new clients. From Moscow. Clients with special needs." Sami looked at the shed.

Rada stood for a moment, and then caught on. She smiled. "When?"

"Soon. Jerzy needs to work out the details and will let me know. A lot of money is involved."

"How much?"

"More than you would think," said Sami. "You would be set, as I would." He looked around. "And you would not be stuck here."

"What about Milos?"

"What about him? I'll just tell him that Elena is doing well and has sent for Sanja." Sami motioned to the shed. "Now let her out of there and be nice to her. Fatten her up a little."

CHAPTER 23

Recon Analysis

Davenport was looking at the photos on the wall of Vlad, Elena, Miri and Chris when Peabody and Washington walked in. Peabody was surprised to see Davenport.

"Interesting cast of characters," said Davenport.

"Yes they are," said Peabody. "We've run down their IDs."

Davenport nodded, and then said to Washington, "how's it working for you so far?"

Washington shrugged his shoulders.

"Everything's fine," said Peabody.

Davenport looked at Peabody. "How can I help?"

"More resources," said Peabody, already knowing the answer.

"Can't do that," he said, "but I'd like to know what's going on. See if there's anything I can do."

Peabody scanned Davenport. "All right," she said. "Here's what we have. Dragovic has something coming in. Something big. From what we know from Interpol about his connections in Albania, Turkey and France, he'll start transporting the heroin soon. Where it enters

North America, we can only guess." Peabody stepped back. "Dragovic's very efficient, and smart."

Peabody stood in front of the pictures, pointing to Miri and Elena. "These women are here illegally, we believe, even though they went through customs at DTW," she said. "Fake passports and visas."

"Why not just pop him on that?" asked Davenport. "He'd be looking at ten to fifteen, minimum."

"We could, and it would probably stick," said Peabody. "But we have bigger fish to fry. We want him, but we want the route back through Europe more," she said. "And the entry point. Detroit, we believe, is a pilot program, so to speak." Peabody tapped the picture of Vlad with the eraser end of a yellow pencil. "If Detroit works, he and whatever associates he has could expand to other, if you don't mind me saying, decaying cities," she said. "Cleveland, Philadelphia, St. Louis, to name a few."

Davenport nodded and looked at the picture of Chris. "Who's this guy?"

"Name is Christopher Wolfe. Works for a limo company," said Peabody. "We shot these at the airport," she said, motioning to the photo of Chris opening the limo door for Vlad, Elena and Miri. "We would have never made a connection if it wasn't for this." She took a small voice recorder from her suit pocket and played the Tiger's Den recording. Peabody pulled the video camera from the black case and showed Davenport the video of Chris and Eddie at the Tiger's Den.

"We couldn't get an ID of who Dragovic was talking to so, so we waited until everyone left," said Peabody.

"We saw him," said Washington pointing to Chris, "and a man in his late fifties in a wheelchair coming out of the room with the bug. We ran the limo driver down," said Washington. "Came up fairly clean. Suspected car thief. Had a juvenile record, but that was expunged," he said. "The guy in the wheel chair is Edward Siegler. Owns a junkyard on the southwest side. Italian Mafia connections, we believe. Auto's been interested in him and his operation for a long time," said Washington. "Suspected chop shop."

Davenport nodded. "Thanks for the update. Again, if there's anything within my power to do to help, just let me know."

CHAPTER 24

Lincoln and Davenport at American

Lincoln looked down at the plate with two conies and a side of fries. He liked American Coney Island better than Lafayette, but knew Davenport didn't. It was almost a religious war in Detroit, those who loved Lafayette and those who loved American.

"The DEA's on this," said Davenport.

Lincoln took a bite of his coney, the onions, chili and mustard dripping off the end of the bun.

"How much do they know?" asked Lincoln.

"They know about your friend, his connections, his women and some limo driver. They know something's coming in, and know it's big," said Davenport.

Lincoln finished his dog and started on another. "How many DEA?" he asked.

"Just one for now, they got nothing hard," said Davenport. "Cool thing is the agent's using one of my men."

"So what do we do?" said Lincoln.

"Watch for now," said Davenport. "They got nothin' real yet, maybe ICE'll be interested at some point about the women and make a bust, but not the DEA." He casually looked around the dining area. "You might want to hold off on that delivery for awhile."

Lincoln thought about how Alanzo would take this. Not good. He would back out immediately and Lincoln wouldn't put it past Alanzo to have him capped, just to cover his tracks. Vlad might also, for that matter.

"No can do," said Lincoln. "The system's been put in motion."

"The system," said Davenport.

"Product's moving and people need to get paid," said Lincoln. "Including you and me."

Davenport looked down at his bowl of chicken soup and grilled cheese sandwich.

Lincoln finished the second dog and fries. "Keep your eyes and ears open, I don't have to say what's at stake," he said. He pushed the empty plate away. "Yes I do. Our motherfucking asses."

"I'll do my best," said Davenport. He wiped his mouth with a paper napkin. This was getting way too loose and sloppy. When things get loose and sloppy people get busted, and capped. He knew- it was his job. Time to nip this shit. Davenport decided to give Vinnie Tucci a call and let him know what's going on. Give him names and get him thinking.

Cletus looked at Davenport's soup and sandwich. "Man," he said. "You at American. Eat something real."

CHAPTER 25

Road Trip

The shipping container came off the freighter in Halifax as Chris and Elena passed through Erie, Pennsylvania. A crate labeled CUSTOM FURNITURE was unloaded, kept in a holding area, cleared through Canadian Customs, stored in a corrugated steel warehouse, picked up by a forklift and loaded on a truck bound for Woodstock, New Brunswick.

By the time the crate would arrive at McLean's Furniture Store in Woodstock, Chris and Elena would be in Houlton, Maine, approximately thirteen miles away.

Chris and Elena stopped for the night at a Howard Johnson in Burlington, Vermont. After a dinner of fried chicken and beer, Chris sat on the bed in the small hotel room. Elena had taken a steady stream of painkillers on the trip, her eyes dull, but her body warm and supple. Chris liked the way she smelled, like a humid, wild violet.

"First thing I'm gonna do is take a shower," said Chris. "Long road trips make me feel greasy."

Chris was too road weary to care whether Elena watched him strip or not. He pulled off his clothes, started the shower and waited for the water to heat up. A bonus, the shower head was surprisingly powerful. He stepped into the shower, letting the hot water wash over his head and face. He put his arms against the wall and stood. The door opened and in walked Elena, naked. She stepped in and embraced him from behind. Chris turned, looked in her eyes, dull but not distant as they usually were. He kissed her, and they made love.

* *

Chris and Elena lay in bed, watching television, Elena's head on Chris's shoulder, her hair still a little wet. Chris felt her tighten, like she suddenly had a severe cramp. She let out a tiny yelp, got up and pulled the bottle of painkillers from her purse. She pulled out a pill and chewed it. Chris watched her.

"You're going to have dump those before we cross the border," he said. "Besides, those are really bad for you."

"I don't care," said Elena. "I need them."

Elena walked over to the bed and got in, sighing as she lay on her back, feeling the wave of relief form the pill pulse through her with every heartbeat. They kept her feelings shielded, like a lion tamer with a whip and a chair. Only the lion grew larger and more powerful while her tools to keep it at bay grew weaker. She sat up, put her face in her hands and began to sob.

"Please don't tell Vlad," she said. "He will kill me."

Chris sat up, startled by Elena's outburst. "Kill you?" he said. "Nobody's going to kill you. What are you talking about?"

"Vlad," she cried. "If he found out I cried in

front of a customer then he would kill me," she said. "That is the system."

"I didn't think I was a 'customer'," said Chris. "System, shit. Everybody has a system. The Government. The Feds. The cops. The Italians. The Albanians. Even we do, at Eddie's. You know what? They don't work. They're all full of holes, and everything eventually falls apart and turns to shit." He looked at Elena. "Why on earth would he want to kill you? He doesn't own you."

"Yes he does," said Elena. "Oh yes he does. He owns several of us. Me. Miri, other girls. He buys us and brings us here. I am not really like this. I hate this," she said.

"Then why do you do it? This is America, for Christ's sake. Get a job somewhere, or go back," said Chris.

"A job," Elena laughed. "That's how all this started. I was tricked, how do you say, duped? Instead of going to Tirana like I was promised I was sold to a pimp. A filthy pimp," she said, sobbing. She looked up at Chris. "And my daughter. My little Sanja. What becomes of her?"

"Your daughter?" said Chris. "You have a daughter? Where is she?"

"At home," said Elena. "With my father and step mother, the evil witch. Her brother is the one who sold me."

"Have you talked to them?"

"No, it is not allowed," she said. "But if I did Vlad would kill me and them if I didn't say everything is fine."

"Didn't you have anyone back home?" asked Chris. "Someone who looks like you surely must have had somebody?"

Elena paused. "I had a husband. Sheptim was his name."

And that's when Elena went away... *She and a young man stood in the town square saying wedding vows under a white arch festooned with red and white flowers. They finished, turned to the guests and were showered with rice and confetti...*

"It was beautiful," she said. "We had the bridal room. I was never happier." Her voice went flat and cold. "Then they came and killed him and damaged me. Many in the army are just gangsters and use that as an excuse to kill people and steal from them."

...Gunshots rang outside in the town square. Sheptim got up and started putting on his underwear and pants. Elena rushed to the window and saw several men lined up and shot by the rebel army. Sheptim tried to lock the door when four rebels burst into the room and tackled him. Elena screamed. Two rebels dragged him from the room, beating him. The other two soldiers went for Elena, slapping her nearly unconscious and throwing her on the bed. Both soldiers raped her, ripping into her, laughing and grunting as they came.

Sheptim was dragged to the town square. The two rebels forced him to his knees.

The soldiers were finished and Elena broke free and rushed to the window, saw Sheptim and screamed his name. He looked up and a rebel strode up to him with a pistol and shot him in the head. Elena saw the surging mist of blood and brains as Sheptim slumped to the ground.

One of the rebels came up behind Elena and knocked her unconscious with a butt of a rifle, and the two rebels raped her again...

"When I woke, I couldn't walk for days. I bled, almost to death. And now I am made to do this," she said, hanging her head.

She looked up at Chris.

"All I want is my daughter," she said. "To take

her and have a life somewhere."

Chris put his arm around her shoulder. "I'm sorry," he said. "I truly am."

Elena curled up to him, like a cat, this warm, naked, trembling woman.

"Please do not tell Vlad," she said.

"Forget it," Chris said. "That's the last thing you have to worry about."

Elena looked at him and smiled faintly. She got up, went to her purse and pulled out a rumpled envelope.

"This is a letter to my father," she said. "I've been too afraid to mail it, but now I don't care. My father must know what happened, so he can protect Sanja."

"Mail it," said Chris. "We can do it tomorrow."

Elena put the letter down, got back into bed and lay close to Chris. "Thank you," she said, the slipped into a deep sleep.

* *

Chris and Elena dropped the letter in a mailbox first thing the following morning.

* *

Chris took the bottle of pills from Elena, pulled off on a dirt road and tossed them into the weeds. "I'm sorry," he said. "But we just can't risk it." Elena looked out the window and wrapped her arms around her.

The morning was bright and cool and Elena wore large Jackie Kennedy sunglasses and an oversized fisherman's sweater, giving her a classic sixties look. Chris ditched his customary black leather jacket for a tan field coat and looked fresh and outdoorsy. Going through Customs was easy just past the border on 95 from Houlton to Woodstock. The guard briefly examined their passports then handed them back.

"Enjoy your stay in Canada," he said.

* *

They found McLean's Furniture Store on Broadway in downtown Woodstock and parked in a small adjacent lot.

"Here we go," said Chris.

They got out of the car and walked toward the front door. "There should be a woman here," said Chris. "I have to say a code phrase, just like in the movies," he said. "She should say a code phrase back, then give us the package. "We'll have a couple of trinkets to take back with us. A vase with some fake flowers and a small globe, with a receipt. Eighty bucks," he said.

They walked in the front door and looked around. Very woodsy and dark. Lamps, sofas, chairs, tables, all with a distinctly northern east coast look and feel. A woman in her sixties was arranging a bin of silky pillows turned when Chris and Elena entered.

"Hello," said the woman. "Can I help you find anything?"

Chris said, "Thanks, we're just looking around. By the way, do you also grow tomatoes here?"

Elena looked at Chris, confused by the illogic. The woman sized them up, Elena still wearing sunglasses.

"Yes we do," she said. "The finest in New Brunswick. Pull your car around back." She turned and disappeared into a back room.

Chris noticed a vase with silk flowers and

globe sitting on a coffee table. "Wait here," he said to Elena.

Chris pulled the car around back to a loading area. The woman came out the rear entrance and waved him back. Chris backed in and got out of the car, looking at a long, rectangular package wrapped in brown, shiny paper secured with duct tape.

"I believe this is what you are looking for," she said.

Chris opened the rear doors, and with some effort unlatched the bottom of the bench seat. The seat cavity was altered to accommodate the package. He loaded in the heroin, heavy and awkward, careful not to puncture and damage any of the individual bundles. He snapped the seat back into place.

"Please take your other items and I will write your receipt," said the woman. Strange accent, thought Chris. Like Elena and Vlad's with the edges worn away. Chris picked up the globe and Elena the vase and followed the woman to a counter with a computer terminal. After a few keystrokes an ink jet printer spit out a receipt. The woman wrapped the small globe in tissue and placed them in an oversized orange shopping bag.

"Goodbye," said the woman. She turned and walked to the silky pillows she was arranging.

Chris and Elena pulled out of the small lot and got back on 95 westbound.

* *

Chris turned right into the Customs Loop on 95 on the American side, just before Airport Drive. He stopped at a booth and rolled down his window and smiled.

"Can I see your identification?" asked the guard.

Chris, already holding their passports, handed them to the guard. The guard examined the passports and looked at Chris and Elena.

"Would you please remove your sunglasses, ma'am." Elena pulled off her sunglasses and looked at the guard. The guard studied their faces, looked into Elena's eyes, and then handed back their passports.

"Do you have anything to declare?" he asked.

"Just these," said Chris, reaching into the back seat and picking up the bag with the vase and globe. He showed them to the guard.

"What was the total amount spent?" he said.

"Eighty dollars," said Chris, pulling out the receipt. "Canadian."

The guard stepped out of the booth. "Please pull over into the inspection area," he said, pointing to a mostly empty lot.

"Is there something wrong?" said Chris. "We just got married and are on our honeymoon. Thought we'd poke around Canada a little, since we've never been up here before," he said.

"Please pull over," said the guard.

Chris pulled into the lot and they sat while the guard walked back to the booth and tapped on a terminal, running the plates. Data popped up on the screen and the guard picked up a phone. The female voice on the other end said, "Plant it and let them pass." Two minutes later he came out of the booth and walked over.

"Could you open the trunk, please?" he said, walking around to the rear of the car.

Shit, thought Chris. Stay calm. By now Chris could read Elena's subtle body language and knew she needed a pill, or a fix. Chris pressed the trunk release button.

The guard looked into the trunk and found it empty and clean. He leaned into the trunk for a moment, out of view. He knelt by the license plate and reached underneath, near the gas tank. He shut the trunk and walked over to the driver's side.

"You're free to go," he said. "Have a nice day."

"Thanks," said Chris. He drove slowly through the loop and turned right onto 95.

The guard picked up the phone and dialed the same number. Peabody asked the guard if he inserted the GPS unit and transponder. The guard responded, "Affirmative."

CHAPTER 26

Clarence on the Down Low

Clarence lay naked in bed with the fifteen year old boy, pissed about the money he lost on the dogfight but happy the kid was with him. He could smell the dogs all the way up here, even in the makeshift attic bedroom.

The kid got out of bed and Clarence admired his slender body, hot little queen if he ever saw one, worth every penny of the fifty bucks he paid him.

Clarence knew the risks of being on the down low, but hey, the kid worked here tending to the dogs, liked Clarence, loved the money and the brother who ran the fights was in the closet himself, so it all worked out.

Clarence was getting hard again when the dogs downstairs and in the yard started barking. The kid went to the window and saw the SWAT team rush up the crumbling cement porch and smash the front door with a steel battering ram. Clarence heard shouting downstairs and shot out of bed. The kid stood naked, still looking out the window, the yard filling up with two squad cars and a black police van.

"Nathan, get your clothes on, godammit," said

Clarence, searching for his underwear and pants.

Fierce barking downstairs followed by a gunshot and a sharp yelp. Clarence heard heavy footsteps trample up the stairs and sat on the bed. The black clothed cops stormed the attic, automatic weapons trained. Clarence saw a red dot dance across his chest.

"On the floor now," shouted one of the cops. Clarence put his hands up. He got on his knees and lay on the floor. One cop stood over him, his foot squarely on Clarence's back, gun pointed at his head.

"You too," said the other cop to the naked kid. The kid complied and lay face first on the stained and dirty blue shag carpet. The cops handcuffed them both with thick nylon ties and did a quick sweep of the room.

"Got any weapons?" said the cop standing over Clarence, pushing his foot into his back.

"No," said Clarence.

"Telling the truth?" said the cop, pressing harder. "Don't lie to me."

"No, man," said Clarence. "I ain't got no motherfucking weapons."

The other cop said to the kid, "How old are you?"

"Eighteen," said Clarence.

"Shut the fuck up," said the cop. "Nobody's taking to you." The cop looked down at the kid. "How old are you?"

"Fifteen," said the kid.

Clarence let out a sigh.

* *

Clarence sat in the interrogation room wearing baggy jeans and a torn white t-shirt. Washington watched him through the one-way glass.

"Caught him naked with an underage boy. Still had a hard on," said Detective Greg Kline, DPD Vice. "Been doing him for awhile, according to the kid. Oral, back door, fifty bucks a pop."

Kline looked at Clarence through the glass. "Dude's an amateur boxer. Used to train at Kronk. Pretty good, too, could go pro. Now he's here looking at ten to fifteen," said Kline. "It's killing him getting caught like this. Worried more about his reputation than the time. This gets out, might as well have a tattoo on his forehead. Step into the ring with that baggage?"

"What does this have to do with me?" said Washington.

"He's talking," said Kline. "He steals cars for a living. Talked about a job coming up at the Marriot, a big one." Kline looked at Clarence through the glass. "This guy's no canary, but he's giving us some useful information. They're going to hit Mercedes, parked in the Millender structure. BMWs also. And get this," said Kline. "Made none other than Cletus B. Lincoln at one of the dogfights, betting pretty heavily, too. Hanging with Alanzo Hendricks. Verified it with the kid, since he was there tending the dogs after the fight."

Washington perked up. "We can bait Millender."

"Thought you would be interested in that," said Kline.

Washington looked at his old partner and smiled. He appreciated the tip. They helped each other out, going back to their Wayne State days.

"What did you offer?" said Washington.

"Contributing, possibly child endangerment," said Kline. "We can't really prove he had sex with the boy, not without some DNA. We can make other charges stick if we try. Found a lot of bud, crack on the premises," said Kline. "Along with the dogs and fifty thousand cash. Turns out the dude running the operation is the kid's second cousin." He turned to Washington. "Want to talk to him?" asked Kline.

"Sure do," said Washington.

* *

Washington sat across from Clarence.

"So when does it go down?" asked Washington.

"Next Saturday night," said Clarence.

"What time?"

"Ten O'clock."

"What's the order?" asked Washington.

"Foreign," said Clarence. "Mercedes M, BMW."

Washington sat back, thinking about where he could get a Mercedes or BMW for bait. "How many?" he asked.

"Four, five if we can," said Clarence.

Washington leaned forward. "Give me some names."

"Can't do that," said Clarence.

"You know what you're looking at," said Washington. "Boxer loves little twinkie boys. There goes any cred you had." He stared at Clarence. "Where's the drop off? Give me names. You cooperate, chances are you may even walk. That's how the system works," said Washington.

Clarence looked at Washington. "I ain't makin' no deal with you. I already did with the other dude. That ain't how this shit works. I wanna talk to a lawyer."

"You don't need a lawyer," said Washington. "What you need right now is me." He stood and looked down at Clarence. "Now," he said. "Here's what you're going to do."

CHAPTER 27

The Delivery

After dropping Elena at the Tiger's Den Chris drove to Eddie's shop per Vlad's instructions. He pulled into the hanger-like garage and Eddie was waiting for him. Chris parked and got out of the car.

"Got the package?" asked Eddie.

"Got it," said Chris. "Where's my hundred grand?"

"Got to get that from Vlad."

"Then why should I give you that package?"

"That was the deal," said Eddie. He frowned. "What's the matter, kid? Don't you trust us?"

"I take all the risk, what did you do?" said Chris.

"Keeping the shit here, ain't I?" said Eddie. "That's a bigger risk than just delivery. He's good for the hundred grand, believe me," said Eddie. "Don't fuck with him, he won't fuck with you." Eddie wheeled closer to Chris. "Besides," he said. "He likes you. He gave you that hot little piece for the ride, didn't he?"

Chris pictured Elena. "That he did."

"He'll be back here tomorrow night," said Eddie. He turned and started wheeling away.

"C'mon," he said. "Get the shit and help me stash it."

Chris went to the car and pulled the package from under the rear seat, getting used to how heavy seventy five pounds felt. He followed Eddie into the back office.

"Move that box," said Eddie, pointing to a wooden box sitting on the floor. Chris gave Eddie a puzzled look, walked over and moved the box, revealing the old in-the-ground safe.

"You talk about trust," said Eddie. "Here's the combination. Spin it to the right to start."

Chris knelt down and looked at the old safe, made of hardened steel, painted dark green like something manufactured in the 1940s.

"Twenty two, fifty four, seventy eight, nineteen," said Eddie slowly.

Chris twirled the combination lock and faintly heard the tumblers click.

"What were the last two?"

"Seventy eight, nineteen," said Eddie.

Chris rotated the dial and at nineteen the tumblers clicked. Chris opened the heavy door. The safe interior smelled musty and stale, like opening a crypt.

"Fits just right, don't it?" said Eddie.

Chris put the package in the safe and fought to keep the combination from slipping from his memory. He associated the numbers-- twenty two and fifty eight, that was easy. That's how old his sister and mother were when his doped out mother drove her car into a tree at seventy miles an hour, killing them both. Seventy eight, that was the year he was born. Nineteen, how old he was when they released him from Juvie.

"Close it up and spin the dial," said Eddie.

Chris spun the dial and stood up and slid the

box over the safe.

"Remember the combination?" asked Eddie.

"Nope," said Chris. "I'm not good at memorizing shit. Twenty two something, forty seven?"

Eddie studied him. "You seen Clarence around?"

"Negative," said Chris. "I've been away, remember? Have you?"

"No. Haven't heard from him either," said Eddie. Which wasn't unusual, they both knew. Clarence would disappear for long stretches-usually after a difficult match. He either recuperated or trained, or so they figured.

He's never missed a boost," said Chris.

Eddie paused. "There's something I gotta tell you," he said. "About the boost."

Chris didn't like the sound of Eddie's voice. "What's that?" he said.

"Paulie's going with you guys."

"What? No fucking way."

"I know how you feel," said Eddie. "But it's business. Good business. Besides, I talked to Zippy and he said he did okay on the Book Cadillac boost."

"No fucking way he's with me," said Chris.

"You, Clarence and Jesus go solo," said Eddie. "Paulie will stick with Zippy."

"Damn straight," said Chris.

"Don't worry about it," said Eddie. "The kid's a little hot under the collar, but he's okay. It'll make Vinnie happy."

* *

Ann Peabody studied the breadcrumb trail on the map on her tablet. Using Google maps she saw the pinpoints through Maine, New Hampshire, New York, Pennsylvania, Ohio then around Lake Erie through Toledo into Detroit, finally stopping and disappearing in the Southwest side. She tapped on the last recorded position, displaying a latitude and longitude value, tapped again and a geocoding engine translated the lat/lon into a street address.

Eddie Siegler's junkyard.

CHAPTER 28

The Millender Boost

Freeman Washington, Ann Peabody, Big Bill Purdy and Walter Robbins sat in the white surveillance van. Peabody sat in the rear bench seat with Robbins. Robbins focused on the laptop display, studying a map showing the location of the bait car in the parking structure along with two unmarked cars, one on Brush and one on Randolph. Both the Larned and Randolph exits were covered.

"Ping the bait," said Washington.

Robbins fiddled with the mouse pad and watched the laptop display.

"Bait's a go," he said.

Washington watched the entrance of the parking structure from the van's front passenger seat. Purdy was in the drivers seat.

"Now we wait," said Washington.

* *

Twenty minutes later Washington saw Clarence wearing a brown nondescript uniform round a corner and slip inside the parking structure. Clarence glanced at the white van.

"There's our mark," said Washington, sitting upright in his seat.

Once in the structure Clarence pulled his gun and walked toward the left booth at the exit gates where the head valet stood and pointed the gun in his face.

"What the…" said the valet, staring at the gun.

"Get in the booth. Now," said Clarence calmly. The valet froze.

"I said get in or die. Choose."

The valet squeezed into the small booth, dropped to the floor and huddled against the corner.

"Stay there, shut the fuck up and don't do anything stupid," said Clarence.

A valet rounded a corner of the parking structure in a silver Lexus and stopped at the booth.

"Where's Leroy?" he said.

"Leroy got fired," said Clarence. "Boss sent me."

The valet, confused said, "But he was just here."

Clarence shrugged. "Don't know nothin' about that. Boss just sent me over." Clarence's hand tightened around the gun.

"God damn," said the valet.

Clarence opened the gate and the valet drove out of the structure and turned on Larned. Clarence pulled a small yellow two way radio from his pants pocket, turned it on and said, "bird's in the nest."

Chris heard it through the static on his end, sitting in the drivers seat of the old but reliable Suburban. "Got it," he replied. He turned to Zippy and Jesus and said, "Alright. This is it."

"Why don't you just use cell phones?" asked

Paulie.

"No record of a call," said Chris. "Can't ID us or put us at the scene. No more questions." He turned and faced Paulie. "Listen up. Stick with Zippy. Do everything he says, watch everything he does and don't say a fuckin' word. Got it?" said Chris.

"Got it man, just like last time," said Paulie. "Chill out. Let's do this."

Chris drove a block closer, pulled the Suburban over and let Zippy and Paulie out.

"Remember what I said," said Chris, pointing at Paulie.

He drove another half block and let Jesus out. Chris then drove around a corner, pulled into an alley, killed the ignition, put the keys under the drivers seat and got out.

* *

Chris walked through the front vehicle entrance, made eye contact with Clarence and walked silently by. Washington watched through a pair of near-field binoculars. "White male entering the structure," he said.

"Can you make him?" asked Peabody.

"No," said Washington.

Zippy and Paulie went in a side entrance and climbed a flight of stairs to the second level. Two valets stood near the key locker, smoking. One started dancing like James Brown and the other laughed as Zippy and Paulie approached. Zippy pulled his 38 and pointed it at the dancing valet.

"Hey, man. What is this?" said the valet.

"Shut the fuck up," said Zippy. "Turn around and walk."

Jesus walked up, gun in hand and covered the

other valet while he rifled through the key locker. He pulled out three keys, two Mercedes, one of them an M class and one BMW.

"Give him your cell phones," said Zippy, motioning to Paulie. The valets handed Paulie their phones.

"Now lie down," said Zippy. "Face first."

The two valets lay on the ground, heads turned, cheeks on the cold, oil-spotted cement. One started whimpering.

"Shut the fuck up, asshole," said Paulie. Zippy gave him a quick look. Them shut up? How about you? Jesus walked over and with two large nylon tie-wraps bound their hands behind their backs. He held his gun to each of the valet's heads, going back and forth, making sure they could feel the barrel against their skulls as he tightened the straps.

Zippy walked over and knelt by the valets. "You make one noise, just one, even when we're gone, I'll know. My friend will know. He's not as nice as me. He will come back and kill both of you."

"Okay, man."

Chris walked up to Jesus. "What we got?"

Jesus handed out the keys, smiling. "Take number ten," he said, handing him the M class keyfob. He handed the other Mercedes fob to Zippy. "Number twenty two," said Jesus. Chris looked at Paulie and pointed to Zippy. "Stick with him," he said.

"This is such a fucking rush, man," said Paulie.

* *

Clarence pulled a different radio from his pocket, much smaller. He pressed a button and said, "It's going down."

Instantly Washington was on the radio. "All units, five-o-three. I repeat. All units, five-o-three."

* *

Zippy and Paulie eased the sleek Mercedes out of the parking space and headed down the exit ramp. They passed the open gate, courtesy of Clarence. Chris started the Mercedes and started driving down the low ceiling structure. Jesus came down in the BMW. Clarence was gone.

Walter Robbins watched the laptop display. The driver's door and ignition indicator lit up and the Mercedes was moving, just exiting the parking structure.

"Fish on," said Robbins.

Before Jesus made the exit Clarence said to the valet, "Have a nice day," turned the corner and walked to the Suburban. He took the keys from under the seat. Three quarters of a tank of gas. He had two thousand cash in his pocket, wondering how far it would take him. Fuck the cops and their deal. Clarence drove away, heading toward Mexico.

"Bait's out," said Robbins, hearing two squad car sirens.

"Kill it," said Washington.

Zippy and Paulie turned right onto Woodward when they heard the sirens and saw the squad cars.

"Holy fuck!" shouted Paulie.

Zippy hit the gas and swerved around a small white delivery truck. He pressed the accelerator all the way to the floorboard but the vehicle slowed. Two squad cars were lit up behind him. The

Mercedes rolled to a stop.

"Fuck me," said Zippy. What were the odds, he thought. Popped. He put his hands on the steering wheel and was already calculating his time. One prior, served five years, but that was when he was a kid. Maybe this time ten to fifteen, depending on the judge. Maybe out in seven, based on good behavior and overcrowding, maybe less if he gave the others up....and he wasn't about to do that.

"This is bullshit," said Paulie. He pulled the 22 pistol from his jacket pocket, swung out the door and aimed the gun at one of the squad cars.

"What the fuck are you doing?" yelled Zippy.

"I ain't going to jail." Paulie fired, pinging one of the squad car's rear view mirror and radiator. Both officers in the other squad car opened their doors, crouched behind them and opened fire. Three shots hit Paulie in the chest, sending him flying back onto the pavement. Another shot passed through the rear windshield and hit Zippy in the left temple and passed through his right. Zippy's eyes blinked once, faded, and went blank. He slumped forward on the steering wheel.

Washington and Purdy jumped from the van with their guns drawn, running toward the blue and whites.

* *

Chris flew out of the structure and sped east on Larned. He saw the squad cars converge on the Mercedes in the rear view mirror. Who was shot? A body was on the pavement. He stepped on the gas and looked in front of him and saw a young woman, crossing Brush at the intersection. He hit her squarely with the left front quarter panel with a bone crushing clunk. The woman pinwheeled through the air and flopped onto the pavement.

"Oh God, no, no," murmured Chris, looking in the rear view mirror. The woman lay crumpled and broken like fresh road kill, blood pooling under her red hair. No movement. Chris went straight on Larned and headed east through an abandoned neighborhood.   He drove for six blocks with the lights off and ditched the car in an open field. He walked in the dark back to his small apartment in the Cass Corridor.

* *

Chris lay on the bed with the lights off, bathed in the cold light of the television, watching the news. A female reporter from Channel 7 stood in front of the Millender Center.

"Two of the car thieves were killed in a shootout with police," said the reporter. "And unfortunately, a young, single mother was killed crossing Brush Street, leaving a five year daughter behind."

Chris sat up.

"If anyone knows or saw any of this go down, please contact the Detroit Police Department immediately," said the reporter. They flashed a photograph of the woman. Pretty, smiling. Red hair and bright green eyes. The segment ended with the camera at the intersection.

Chris put his head in his hands, just wishing to God he could take it all back, that it didn't happen. He just killed an innocent woman. With a kid. It rolled over and over in his mind, and didn't seem real. But it was.

He got up and pulled a large duffel bag from a

closet and started packing clothes. Underwear, socks, shirts, whatever was clean, and his cash. He was done with Detroit, and it was only twenty-four hours to Florida.

CHAPTER 29

Party Time

Miri and Elena stood in front of Vlad's desk in the back office of the Tiger's Den. The door was shut, music leaking through. Cletus B. Lincoln sat on a couch perpendicular to the desk.

"Both of you are going to a party tonight," said Vlad.

"Where at?" asked Miri.

"A place my friend has arranged," said Vlad, motioning to Lincoln.

"Hello ladies," said Lincoln, smiling.

"What kind of party is it?" asked Elena.

"One that will be lots of fun," said Lincoln, looking Elena up and down. "A very important person will be there," he said.

"We are very discreet," said Miri.

"I bet you are."

"Go get your jackets," said Vlad.

Elena and Miri walked out of the office.

"Take the older one," said Vlad. "Trust me. She will do anything."

* *

Elena and Miri entered the large house two

blocks off the west side of Woodward. Lincoln rented it at the beginning of the Mayor's second term. They walked through the large foyer and into the great room. A few empty glasses and bottles littered the tables and by the oak fireplace mantle. The air was stale with residual cigarette, cigar and a minute trace of marijuana smoke.

Miri and Elena followed Lincoln into a back room, a library, with books stacked on mahogany shelves reaching to the ceiling. The classic library, left by the owners, was furnished with a large desk, an oversize leather reading chair and a dark leather sofa.

"This is the one I was telling you about," said Lincoln, putting his arm around Elena. "Happy birthday."

The Mayor of Detroit looked Elena up and down.

"Very nice, very nice," he said. The Mayor motioned toward Elena. "Come here and sit down next to me." Elena walked over and sat close to the Mayor. He looked at Lincoln and Miri. Lincoln smiled. "See you later," said the Mayor.

Lincoln, stung by the abrupt brush-off, grabbed Miri's arm and walked out of the library.

"Shut the door please," said the Mayor. He scanned Elena. "You're a very beautiful woman."

"Thank you"

"I like the way you talk," said the Mayor. "It's sexy. European." He paused. "Do you know who I am?"

"No," said Elena.

The Mayor laughed. "That's a first," he said. "That's good. Let me just say that I have a busy schedule and a wife who is not very accommodating."

"I'm sorry to hear that," said Elena.

"Don't be," said the Mayor. "We just have a little arrangement. She goes about her business and I go about mine. Discretely." He smiled. "Kind of a don't ask don't tell policy."

The Mayor put his hand between Elena's legs and slowly moved it up. Elena tightened at the initial contact, then relaxed, wishing she had taken a painkiller. She had cut down almost to nothing, thinking about Sanja and bolstered by the slim chance that Milos would read the letter she sent. He might get to read it if Rada didn't get her filthy hands on it first. She opened her legs. "That's it, baby," said the Mayor, then he kissed her.

* *

Lincoln led Miri up the winding stairs. She ran her hand along the massive oak bannister and Lincoln took her into a dimly lit bedroom. He sat on the bed.

"I want you to do exactly what I like," he said.

Miri shrugged. "I am up for anything."

"Take off your clothes."

Surprised at such a mundane request, Miri said, "sure." She slipped out of her dress and stood nude.

"Nice," said Lincoln. He patted the bed. "Come here."

Miri slowly strolled over and sat next to Lincoln. Lincoln stood and took off his clothes, tossing them on an easy chair. He started kissing and fondling Miri. She moaned, her eyes open, staring at a wall.

"You like that baby? You like that?" said Lincoln. He pushed Miri down on the bed, got on top of her and entered her. Miri loosened and Lincoln put one of his large hands around her throat and squeezed.

"Try this, baby," he said softly. "This turns me on so much…"

Miri gasped and Lincoln let up, allowing her to breathe.

"Please," said Miri. "Not so hard. I cannot breathe."

"That's the point, baby," said Lincoln. "Heightens the experience. For both of us."

Lincoln drove it hard into Miri, moaned and wrapped his right hand around Miri's throat and then held her arms behind her head with his left. He squeezed her throat and pumped harder. Miri choked, the started flailing.

"That's it, that's it baby," said Lincoln. "Feel it? Feel good?" Lincoln pumped and squeezed harder, her throat and neck so soft, so flexible. He closed his eyes.

Miri went limp and turned blue as Lincoln finished. He rolled over. "That was good, baby. That was so good," he said. He looked at Miri, not breathing.

"Hey," he said. He shook Miri, and then shook her again. "Hey! Oh shit, oh shit," said Lincoln, looking around the room. "Fuck me, fuck me, Jesus." He scrambled from the bed and dressed. He stood in front of the bed, looking down at Miri's body, her eyes wide open. He picked up her dress and put it on the bed. Thinking for a moment, he then wrapped Miri in the loose bedspread. Lincoln pulled his cell phone from his pocket and called the Mayor.

* *

The Mayor, finished with Elena, sat back on the sofa in his boxer shorts and lit a cigar. Elena was dressed, except for her shoes. The Mayor's cell phone rang. He looked at the number, frowned and answered.

"Yes?" he said. "You know I don't like being disturbed when I'm with a lady."

"I know, I know. We gotta problem."

"And what would that be?"

"With one of the hos," said Lincoln.

"What kind of problem?" said the Mayor.

"A big one."

The Mayor took the phone from his ear and sneered at it. He was just about done with Lincoln, had been for a long time. This was the capper. "This sounds like something I shouldn't be hearing," he said.

"I'm not sure what to do," said Lincoln.

Alarmed, the Mayor thought Lincoln always knew what to do and always kept a clear, cool head. When the time a deranged laid off city bus driver came at him with a kitchen knife Lincoln stepped in cool and calm. Took fifteen stitches, but he took out the dude with the knife in a fat hurry.

"This sounds serious," said the Mayor.

"It is," said Lincoln. "Bad serious." His voice was shaky.

He should have known better, Lincoln with all his kinky shit.

"Look, goddammit," said the Mayor. "Don't tell me nothin' I don't need to know. Just clean up what you messed up," he said. "And keep me out if it. Understand?"

"Okay, okay," said Lincoln, thinking. "The other ho still with you?" he asked.

"Yes. And I never saw her tonight. Clear?"

"I know that," said Lincoln. "I need to get her out of here. You done with her?"

"Sounds like I am now," said the Mayor.

"I'll be by to pick her up in a couple of minutes."

"Alright." He terminated the call and looked at Elena. "It looks like you're leaving in a few."

Elena put on her shoes and smiled nervously, wishing she had a painkiller. She walked toward the front door.

* *

Lincoln left Miri wrapped in the bedspread, hustled down the stairs, through a side door onto a circular driveway. He got in the black city issued Tahoe and pulled close to the side door, then got out and opened the lift gate.

Lincoln went back into the house through the side door and carried Miri down the stairs. He put her in the cargo area of the Tahoe, shut the gate, turned and walked toward the front door of the grey stone house.

Elena stood at the door watching Lincoln. He stopped abruptly.

"Get in the car," he said.

"Where is Miri?" asked Elena.

"Don't worry about her. Just get in the car."

"What did you put in the back?" said Elena. "Where is Miri?"

"I told you not to worry about her. Get in the front seat," he said, anger rising in his voice.

Elena walked toward the car, cautiously with Lincoln right behind her. Instead of opening the passenger's door she opened the rear door and peered into the cargo area. The top of Miri's head was exposed, her red hair flowing out of the bedspread. Elena bolted back right into Lincoln.

"I told you to get in the front seat," he said.

He grabbed Elena's arm, slammed the rear door shut, opened the front, turned Elena and held her by the hair, forcing her into the front seat.

Elena fought back. "What have you done to Miri?" she screamed.

"Shut up, bitch," said Lincoln. He hit her and her head snapped forward. She raged back and gouged Lincoln's face with her nails, one of the false nails breaking off near Lincoln's eye.

Lincoln cried out and put his hand over his eye. Elena broke free and ran down the brick driveway and onto the street. Lincoln righted himself and walked after Elena, still holding his hand over his eye. Elena ran to a nearby house, pounded on the door and started screaming. Lincoln rushed up behind her. Elena saw him and ran across the large lawn toward Woodward. The world changed when Elena sprang onto Woodward Avenue. Open fields, burned out houses and broken, iron-barred storefronts.

Elena ran down Woodward toward the massive green Renaissance Center in the distance and ducked in a small alley between two derelict storefronts. She hid behind an open trash dumpster.

* *

Lincoln ran out toward Woodward looking for Elena, guessing where she would go. He picked the direction toward downtown and walked. He walked for a block and weighed the risk of not finding her versus someone, especially the Mayor, finding Miri in the back of the Tahoe. He could always deal with the bitch later. Through Vlad. He turned and walked back to toward the house.

* *

Lincoln drove down Woodward toward Hart Plaza and turned left on Jefferson Avenue. He drove past the Millender Center, beyond the RenCen toward the warehouse district near Belle Isle. He drove two miles, stopping at every red light, then turned right onto the MacArthur Bridge. He turned left on Sunset and stopped in the parking area at the end of Pleasure Drive.

Lincoln stepped out of the Tahoe and opened the lift gate. He pulled Miri from the rear of the Tahoe and carried her to the shore. He unwrapped her from the blanket and rolled her into the river, jumping back from the splash. Miri bobbed and was immediately caught in the strong downriver current. She sank in the cold water, then partially surfaced, her left arm and red hair visible. She sank again as the murky water rushed in her open mouth.

Lincoln knew she would stay at the bottom of the river for a day or so. Maybe more. The cold current would carry her down the river and into the deep Fleming shipping channel. He took the blanket and tossed it in the Tahoe, closed the lift gate and drove back across the MacArthur Bridge and back down Jefferson toward Woodward, determined to find Elena.

CHAPTER 30

Lincoln on the Hunt

Elena emerged from behind the dumpster, shivering from the cold. She walked cautiously going south on Woodward, stopping in front of a storefront with the words Motor City Mission hand painted on a plywood sign. There were lights on inside and she saw people sitting on chairs and makeshift benches, some wrapped in blankets.

Elena opened the heavy door and walked in slowly, looked around and saw an open wooden folding chair near a clanking radiator. She sat in the chair and shivered, absorbing the radiator's heat.

A short black man in worn preacher clothes saw her as soon as she walked in the door. He strolled over to Elena, looking her up and down. He'd seen a tidal wave of hookers during his time at the mission- meth hoochies, crack whores, smack addicts, some formerly from the suburbs, all with the same hollow, vacant look. All with bad teeth. This one certainly was different.

"My, my," he said. "Who are you? Where did you come from?"

Elena sat with her arms wrapped around her, shivering.

"Looks like you could use a blanket," said the Preacher. He walked to a storage cabinet and pulled out a coarse green army surplus blanket and wrapped it around her.

"Thank you," said Elena.

"You're welcome. Sorry about the blanket, but that's all we have," he said. "What are you doing here?"

"I had an accident," said Elena.

"Accident? Did you call the police?" he asked.

"No. No police, please." Elena looked up at the Preacher.

The Preacher looked at her suspiciously. "All right," he said. "No police."

"Do you have a telephone I could use?" said Elena. She had Chris's cell number burned in her memory.

"Let's see now," he said, crossing his arms and stroking his graying goatee with his fingers. "That's really against the rules, lending my phone out. I shouldn't do this," he said. "By protocol I should call the police and report you. You didn't have no accident."

"Please," said Elena. She gazed up at him, eyes pleading. She felt a sharp pain in her head and her skin began to itch. She shivered, a deep tremor running through her from withdrawal and the cold.

The Preacher watched her shake, and pulled a thin, older cell phone from his pocket. "Tell the truth, the police been nothin' but trouble for me," he said. "Here." He flipped open his phone and held it out to Elena.

Elena looked at the phone. "Please," she said. "I don't know how to use that kind."

The Preacher, surprised, said "Say what? You can't use a cell phone? Girl, what planet you from?"

"Could you please dial for me?" she asked.

The Preacher shrugged. "I guess so," he said.

Elena said the number slowly and the Preacher dialed and held the phone to his ear. Hearing it ring he handed the phone to Elena.

＊ ＊

Chris was looking at his road atlas, flipping through the map pages from Detroit to Miami. Straight shot down I-75 all the way. His cell phone rang, startling him. He answered on the fourth ring, not recognizing the number.

"Hello?" he said.

"Chris, Chris," cried Elena. "Oh God, please help me. It's Elena."

"Hey, calm down," he said. "What's the matter?"

"Miri. It's Miri. Help me. I don't know where I am," she said. "He's trying to kill me. Please come get me."

The Preacher frowned.

"Wait a minute," said Chris, looking at his packed duffel bag. "Slow down. What's going on? Who's trying to kill you?"

"It's Miri. Please come get me before he does," said Elena.

"Okay, okay," said Chris. "Where are you?"

Elena looked up at the now stern-faced Preacher.

"Where is this? Please."

"This is the Motor City Mission on Woodward," said the Preacher. "By the New Center."

"Mission, Motor," said Elena. "Woodward. New Center."

"I know where that is," said Chris.

"Hurry," said Elena. "Please hurry."

"Just sit tight," said Chris. "I'm on my way."

* *

Chris pulled in front of the mission. Elena, standing at the front door, turned and briefly took the Preacher's hand. "Thank you, thank you," she said. She ran out to the street toward Chris on the Harley.

"What the hell is going on?" said Chris.

"Vlad," said Elena. "He made us go to a party, but it wasn't a party. Only two of them there. One of them was very important. The other, he killed Miri." Elena buried her face in her hands and started crying. "Then he tried to kill me."

"What?" said Chris. "Who was it? Who tried to kill you?"

"His name is Lincoln, I think. I don't remember names so well," she said. "All I know is he is a friend of Vlad's."

"Who was the other guy, the important one?" said Chris.

"I don't know," said Elena, shivering. She looked at Chris and held on to her arm. Chris took off his leather jacket and gave it to her.

"I cannot go back to Vlad," she said. "Please."

"Don't worry about it," said Chris. "Stay with me."

"Do you mean that?" she said.

"Sure. At least until we can figure this thing out. Hop on," he said.

Elena held on to Chris as they tooled down Woodward toward the Cass Corridor.

* *

Lincoln cruised down Woodward in the black Tahoe driving slowly in the right lane, guessing where Elena could have gone. He stopped and parked on the west side of Woodward. If she went south she would have ducked into any safe place she could have just to get out of the cold and the drizzle.

Simple time and distance, he figured.

He got out of the car and walked toward the RenCen, looking into the abandoned storefronts, through the black wrought iron gates covering the broken windows and doors. Lincoln stopped in front of the only place that had any signs of life- the Motor City Mission. He walked inside.

The Preacher saw him. "Can I help you?"

"I hope so," said Lincoln. "I'm looking for someone."

"Oh?" said the Preacher.

"Yes," said Lincoln. "A woman. White. Foreign accent. Might have passed through here last night."

"I see," said the Preacher. "We usually don't discuss the people we help here. Privacy and the law, unless you're a police officer." The Preacher looked at Lincoln. "Are you with the police?"

"No," said Lincoln. "This is a private matter."

"Then I can't really say anything," said the Preacher. "I'm sure you understand."

Lincoln nodded and looked around. "You get much support here?" he asked.

"Not as much as we'd like."

"What about support of a more personal nature?"

"Very, very little, unfortunately."

Lincoln pulled a hundred dollar bill from his pocket.

"I'd like to make a donation, brother," he said, handing the bill to the Preacher.

"This is much appreciated," said the Preacher, taking the bill and putting it in his pants pocket.

"Like I said, a white woman," said Lincoln. "Foxy, dark hair. Exotic."

"A white woman?" said the Preacher. "Oh, yes. Was in here last night. Had a hard time understanding her," he said. "Hardly had anything on."

"What happened?"

"She was scared to death. She said she had an accident, but I didn't buy that for a minute. She talked about someone, Mirror, Miriam, something like that. Kept on saying her name," said the Preacher.

"Oh yeah?" said Lincoln. "Is she still here?"

"No. Some white dude picked her up. On a motorcycle."

Lincoln nodded. "How did she get a hold of him?"

"I let her use my phone," said the Preacher.

"Still got the number she called?"

"Might still be in my cell phone."

"Can I see it?"

The Preacher smiled and looked at Lincoln's pocket.

Lincoln looked squarely at the Preacher. "In my experience," he said, "there's always something goin' on in a place like this. Runnin' hos, gambling, fencing shit, whatever. Someone's always dealing something out the back door. Got some friends at the DPD," said Lincoln. "And City Hall. One phone call…"

The Preacher looked up at Lincoln, pulled out his cell phone and handed it to him.

Lincoln flipped open the phone and

navigated to the dialed calls. There was only one listed. Lincoln wrote down the number and looked at the call's time stamp: 12:45pm. He flipped the phone shut and handed it to the Preacher.

"You've been very helpful," said Lincoln. "And I was never here."

* *

Lincoln drove in the Tahoe and called Andre Davenport. Davenport answered.

"Hey," said Lincoln.

"Hey yourself," said Davenport. "Sup?"

"I need a little favor."

"Oh? What's that?" said Davenport.

"Can you run a phone number for me?"

"Cell or land line?" said Davenport.

"Don't know."

Davenport grabbed a pen and a scrap of paper. "Doesn't matter. Shoot."

Lincoln rattled off the number and turned left on Randolph, toward City Hall.

"Call you back," said Davenport.

CHAPTER 31

Miri Washes Up

The two little girls, six and eight, were playing where they shouldn't, near the canal seawall below the dock. There were fun things to do there, especially when they brought their dolls. Sometimes they could see little fish being chased and eaten by bigger fish. Their dolls would be pirate princesses, threatened by sharks. Sometimes they saw bright green frogs and thought if their dolls kissed them the frogs would turn into princes, but they could never quite catch one.

They walked to the rear of the deep, neatly mowed lot behind the massive Grosse Ile three-story white stucco house. It was an easy climb down the dock ladder to the narrow strip of sandy shore. The older girl went last, looking back at the house. Their mother was inside on the phone, and would be for at least an hour. She always was on the phone and hated to be bothered. Plenty of time for the pirate princesses to explore and pretend...

They first saw the red hair, matted and tangled, thick as a rope. They looked at the swollen body, bloated and gray, eyes open, black and looking at them but seeing nothing. The younger girl screamed and ran to the ladder. The older girl backed away, bumped against the seawall and jumped a foot in the air. Both girls ran toward the house.

* *

Ann Peabody was shocked at the number of

unclaimed bodies at the Wayne County Morgue, so much so she made a comment to the assistant medical examiner.

"I've been around," she said. "But I've never seen bodies stacked like this." She looked at Washington. "Not even in New York."

"Business as usual," said the examiner, dressed in a white lab coat and regulation green scrubs. "Even the storage rooms where we keep chemicals and cleaning supplies are full," he said. "Gets to be a real problem in the summer, keeping them cold."

Peabody knew the smell. There was no mistaking the smell of death- it was always the same, only to different degrees. Peabody smelled an excess of death here.

They followed the examiner to the main morgue, then to drawer twenty one.

"Twenty one," said the examiner. "Jane Doe." He pulled the drawer all the way out and pulled the gray sheet back revealing Miri.

Peabody stared down at her. She must have been pretty once, natural red hair, green eyes, now lifeless. One finger missing.

"Cause of death appears to be strangulation," said the examiner. "Two little girls found her washed up on Grosse Ile, right in their back yard. What a shocker for a couple of rich kids."

"Time of death?" asked Peabody, still staring at Miri.

"Looks like a little over twenty four hours ago. Approximately," said the examiner. "Best guess. When we find them in the water it can go either way, plus or minus a day or two, depending on the state of the body."

"Positive on the cause?" asked Washington. He thought about the bank president who disappeared a few years ago. Found him two weeks later. After the autopsy, the coroner officially reported the cause of death as drowning. A private autopsy showed he took a bullet to the base of the skull. How the hell did they miss that?

"Certainly appears that way," said the examiner. "Bruises on the neck, crushed esophagus. Didn't breath in any water. It seeped in. She was dead before being dumped in the river."

CHAPTER 32

Chris and Elena

Elena, deeply chilled from riding on the back of the Harley, stood in the shower for a long time. Chris watched her through the half-open door and opaque shower curtain. He sat at a small kitchen table, the television on, counting the TradeWind money. One hundred and twenty five thousand wasn't nearly enough, but it didn't seem important now.

What was the woman's name? What was she like? What was her daughter's name? How was the little girl feeling- right now? Who would take care of her? Chris sat blankly staring at the television, in his mind seeing the woman hit the car. Split second eye contact, then clunk. Slow hard bone yielding against harder, faster metal. Pinwheeling, lying dead in the street…and he killed her. Killed her. Chris Wolfe killed her.

Elena walked into the living area of the small studio apartment, naked, drying her hair with a towel. Chris looked at her.

"Feeling any better?"

"Yes, thank you." She sat on the bed next to him. "No. Not really," she said, the skin on her arms and legs forming goose bumps. Elena shivered and scratched her itchy flesh, feeling like insects were crawling inside her.

"I need a pill," she said.

Chris got up and walked to the bed. He sat and put his arms around her. When was the last time a beautiful, naked woman sat on his bed? He couldn't remember, but it didn't matter. The last thing he felt like was sex.

"I'm going to Florida," he said, looking at her. "Come with me." He hugged her, his cheek to hers.

"I cannot," she said.

Chris pushed back and looked at her. "Why not? We can ditch this fucked up life and maybe have a real one."

"You would want me?" said Elena.

"Yes I would. And I do."

"After all the men?" She looked away. "I'm used. Damaged."

"That doesn't matter. How can I hold something against you that you were forced to do?"

Elena smiled and shook, her muscles cramping. Chris held her.

"You can beat this," he said. "You're tough and strong. Stronger than you think."

"You are so kind to me," she said. She looked up at him. "I love you. But I can't do it. Not without my Sanja. I think about her every minute. I want to go home, no matter what happens."

Chris stood. He looked at the bag of money. Money. What was it? Freedom? Power? Maybe it could buy Elena a ticket home, and happiness.

"I already destroyed one family," he said, staring at the television. "Forever. It's my fault, and I have to live with that. I'm not sure if I can." He looked down at Elena. "Maybe I can help fix yours."

"How?" said Elena.

Chris thought, reasoning it out. First, a plane ticket. Eddie was always on the Internet, surfing porn. They could go to Eddie's and buy Elena a ticket on-line. One way to Frankfurt or Athens. They could print the boarding pass right there. From Athens she could get to Tirana. Vlad fucked up- Elena still had her passport from the road trip. He would split his money with Elena. Hell, give her most of it. He'd keep fifty thousand and give her the rest. Ninety five thousand could keep her going for a while. Elena could hook up with her daughter and meet him in Florida. Maybe be a real family. He would need Eddie's help and have to square things with Vlad. Then he would wait for Elena's call.

"We need to go see Eddie," said Chris. "He may be able to help us figure out things with Vlad. Convince him to let you go."

Elena held the hairbrush and glanced at the television, not wanting to get her hopes up, just to have them shattered. Chris kept Channel 2, 4 or 7 on almost always for local news. Channel 7 was on. The Mayor of Detroit stood in front of the green Spirit of Detroit sculpture at the side of the Coleman Young Municipal Building, talking to reporters about more cuts to the city bus service. Elena's eyes widened. "That's him!" That's who Vlad made me be with."

Cletus B. Lincoln stood to the left, a short distance back, talking on a radio.

Elena dropped the hairbrush. "Look! That's the man that killed Miri!" She rushed to the television and pointed. "That's who's trying to kill me."

Chris looked at the TV. "Don't you know who

that is? That's the Mayor of Detroit," he said. "The other guy, I've seen him around. He's the Mayor's security guy. Like his personal bodyguard." He looked at Elena, her gaze frozen on the television.

"This is not good," said Chris.

CHAPTER 33

Eddie's Out

Eddie was taking a piss when Vinnie walked into the office carrying a large plastic bag full of cut up onions and a roll of duct tape. Eddie zipped up, motored out of the can and stopped when he saw Vinnie.

"Vinnie, we gotta talk," said Eddie, seeing and smelling the onions.

"I get a call," said Vinnie quietly. "Cop I know. Well placed. He's says you're hooked up with the Albanian I've been looking for. DEA's after him too."

Eddie looked at Vinnie, then down at the shop floor.

Vinnie pulled his Beretta 8000, pointed it at Eddie's head. "He said that the DEA and the cops knew about the Marriot boost. That's how it got stung."

Eddie gripped the armrests on his wheelchair.

"You should have seen Paulie's mother," said Vinnie. "My sister. At the funeral. She's ruined. Done. First her husband, now her son. My nephew." He looked down at Eddie. "All because of you."

Vinnie held the Beretta to Eddie's temple and

ripped of a piece of duct tape with his teeth. He taped Eddie's arm to the chair.

"What the fuck are you doing?" said Eddie. "Wait a minute. Yeah, I engineered a couple of boosts with him but that's it."

"How come I don't believe you?" said Eddie. He taped Eddie's other arm to the chair.

"Look," said Eddie. "I'm sorry about Paulie. I really am. But my guy Zippy's dead, too. Paulie pulled a gun and started shooting. Zippy's dead because of him."

Vinnie hit Eddie in the jaw with the Beretta handle. Eddie cried out, blood pouring from his mouth. He slowly spat out two molars.

"You think I give a shit about that stupid spick?"

"C'mon, man," said Eddie. "What do you want me to do? I can't bring him back. It just went south."

"Went south," said Vinnie. He put the Beretta in his pocket, opened the bag of onions and put it over Eddie's head, holding the bag around Eddie's neck. Eddie screamed, the sound muffled by the bag.

The vapor from the onions hit Eddie like a freight train. He instantly choked, unable to breathe. He held his breath until his reptile brain took over and inhaled deeply, the powerful onion vapor filling his lungs and burning his esophagus. Eddie's arms and torso stiffened, like a man in a gas chamber. His head dropped and he started to pass out.

Vinnie pulled the bag from Eddie's head, dropping onion fragments on Eddie's lap. He gasped for air.

"Just like the old days," said Vinnie. "Brings back memories, don't it?" He held the bag of onions and shook it. "Now. Tell me what else you got going with the Albanian."

"Just a couple of boosts," Eddie whispered. "That's it."

"Bullshit," said Vinnie. He took the bag and put it over Eddie's head from behind. Eddie shook his head from side to side as Vinnie taped the bag around Eddie's neck. Eddie's mouth moved.

"What's that?" said Vinnie. "I can't hear you?" He pulled the Beretta from his belt. "You want to tell me something?"

Eddie nodded. Vinnie ripped the duct tape from the bag and Eddie's neck, pulling skin with it.

"What you got to say?"

Eddie's head bobbed. Barely conscious, he looked up at Vinnie.

"Fuck you." Eddie's head dropped.

Vinnie smiled. "Okay," he said. "Have it your way." He put the Beretta to Eddie's temple and pulled the trigger. Eddie's head reeled to the left from the impact. The entrance hole was small, much smaller than the exit wound. Blood, skull fragments and brains sprayed on the walls and floor. One lump of gray matter landed on the side of the box that covered the floor safe.

Vinnie pocketed the Beretta, took a look at Eddie slumped in the chair, turned and strolled out.

CHAPTER 34

Diamonds and Blood

"What's that smell?" said Elena as she and Chris entered the chop shop.

"Onions," said Chris, frowning.

They walked through the garage to the office, the onion smell getting stronger. They walked in the office and saw Eddie, dead, strapped to the wheelchair, the small room filled with cut up onions, blood and brains. Elena instantly turned and retched.

"Jesus Christ," said Chris. He walked over to Eddie, holding his nose to his sleeve, trying to mask blood and onions odor. Vlad must have done this. Eddie must have fucked him somehow. Chris went to the floor safe, the rug covered by blood and a lump of brains. He kicked the brains out of the way and moved the box, exposing the floor safe. He sat on his haunches, trying to remember the combination. If it was Vlad, chances are the safe was empty and they were done.

"Can you open it?" asked Elena, nearly choking.

"I think so," said Chris. Think. Calm down. Just like a boost. Be systematic. If he could get the first number, the rest would fall in place. What was the association?

"Twenty two," he said, conjuring an image of his mother and sister. "Twenty two." Chris spun the tumbler and stopped on twenty two. "Fifty eight," he said and positioned the dial to fifty eight, hearing the faint tick of the tumblers. "Seventy eight and nineteen."

The lock clicked and released. Chris pulled open the door.

The bags of dope were in the canvass bag. Chris counted ten of them. Sitting on top was a small black velour sack.

"It wasn't Vlad," said Chris. "Holy shit, it wasn't Vlad." He looked up at Elena.

"We got to get out of here, fast," said Chris. "He's going to come here and get his dope. He could be on his way, right now."

Chris pulled the heroin from the safe, careful not to set it on the blood and brains." He picked up the velour sack and peered in. He looked at Elena then back in the bag. "Diamonds," he said. "Eddie talked about converting cash into gold or diamonds, but I thought it was only talk." He looked at the icy clear rocks in the bag and handed it to Elena. "Here," he said. "Take these. Keep them." Chris walked around the desk and turned on Eddie's computer. It was older, and used a dial up modem for the Internet, but at least he had an ink jet printer. Chris moved fast but the computer didn't.

"Come on, goddammit," he said. The computer finally booted and Chris clicked the browser icon and navigated to Delta Airlines. He checked the flights to Frankfort, Germany and Athens, Greece. Greece was a better bet. There was a flight leaving in two hours with three seats available. He walked over to Eddie's body and pulled Eddie's wallet from his sweat pants pocket. It was wet with onion juice and traces of blood. He pulled out a MasterCard.

Back at the computer Chris bought a ticket from DTW to Athens, one way, and typed in Eddie's card numbers. A moment later, a confirmation came up on the screen, verifying a boarding pass. He turned on the small ink jet printer by the side of the computer and printed the pass.

The printer spit out the boarding pass and Chris handed it to Elena.

"Here," he said. "This will get you to Athens. From there you can get back home. Take the diamonds. They're a lot easier to hide than cash. I have no clue how much they're worth, but it's gotta be a lot."

Elena took the boarding pass and the diamonds. "Come with me," she said. "Please come."

"I can't. There's no way. I have to fix things with Vlad," he said.

Chris hefted up the canvas bag, the parcels of heroin shifting with gravity. "We gotta get out of here and get you on that plane. We'll take one of Eddie's cars."

* *

Thirty minutes later Vlad pulled up and walked into the garage. He saw Eddie and the open safe door.

CHAPTER 35

The Letter Arrives

Milos was home early, his arthritis acting up. Rain tapped at the windshield. He stopped by the mailbox in his rickety Lada Niva and saw the letter from the United States, addressed only to him. The address was written in Elena's handwriting. Instead of driving up to the cottage and taking the mail inside he sat in the small truck and opened the letter.

Dearest Papa,

I am a slave here. I was sold by Sami to a person named Jerzy who owns a sex club. I was then bought by a man named Vlad and taken to America. I have been made to do terrible things. I am so ashamed. Rada knew. Please, please take care of Sanja and keep her away from Rada and Sami. I love you and miss you, and I'm determined to come home one day.

Elena

Milos looked at the letter for a long time, letting it sink in. He neatly refolded it, put it in the envelope and put it in his coat pocket. He drove up the driveway. Rada stood at the door.

* *

Inside, Milos walked past Rada to a closet and pulled out his shotgun.

"Stop," said Rada. "Are you crazy?"

Milos said nothing. He picked up the double barrel shotgun, opened the chamber and filled it with two shells.

"What are you doing?" said Rada, alternately looking at the gun and Milos's robotic expression.

Milos snapped the barrel shut. He reached in his coat pocket and handed Rada the letter. Rada took it, read it and recoiled when she saw Elena's handwriting.

"Please," she said. "I had nothing to do with this. It was all Sami."

"Read it."

Rada opened the envelope and read the letter, stopping at the line, *Rada knew. Please, please take care of Sanja and keep her away from Rada and Sami.* She looked up at the shotgun, pointed at her face.

"You knew this," said Milos. "You knew this all along." Milos looked around. "Where is Sanja?"

"It's not true," said Rada. "It was Sami, not me."

"Where is Sanja?" Milos cocked the trigger on one of the barrels.

Rada looked down. "In her room," she said. "Sleeping."

Milos nudged her with the shotgun. "Out," he said, motioning to the door with the shotgun. "Now. If I ever see you again, I will kill you."

"But Milos, it was Sami. All Sami. What was I to do?"

"Now," said Milos.

Rada hung her head and walked toward the bedroom room. "I will pack my bag," she said.

"I don't think you understand," said Milos. "I said now. As you are. Move."

"Like this? It's freezing outside." Rada started walking in circles.

"I have never hit a woman," said Milos. "But I swear, if I put this shotgun down I will beat you to death. Now go." Milos put the shotgun to Rada's face. "I never want to see you, hear from you, or hear about you again. If I ever see you, I will kill you." He nudged her toward the front door, opened it and pushed Rada out. Rada stood on the cold gravel, looked back at the cottage, then turned and faced the rain.

*   *

An hour later Milos checked the grounds, holding the shotgun. There was no sign of Rada. He went inside, woke Sanja and told her to get dressed and put her coat on. They drove into the village to a public telephone.

"Wait here," said Milos. "I have to make a call." Milos left the truck running. He stepped into the phone booth and dialed Sami's cell phone number.

"Halo?" said Sami.

"Sami. This is Milos. It's Rada. She is very sick. I don't know what's wrong with her. She's been asking for you."

"What is wrong?" said Sami.

"I don't know, but it's very serious. I'm afraid to move her in my truck. Maybe you can help with your big car."

"I will come right away," said Sami. Milos could almost feel the worry in Sami's voice.

CHAPTER 36

Dodge City at DTW

Cletus B. Lincoln looked at the number for the incoming call and answered. Andre Davenport said, "I ran down that number for you. It belongs to one Christopher Wolfe."

"Got an address?" said Lincoln.

Davenport gave him the address. "Cass Corridor. Apartment building, right on the corner of Cass and Ferry."

"I know where that is," said Lincoln. "Right across from the party store. Down by Wayne State."

"That's right," said Davenport.

"Thanks, dog," said Lincoln. "I owe you one."

"Just don't involve me."

* *

Lincoln pulled over on Cass, in full view of the two-tone gray Victorian apartment building. He picked up his cell phone and dialed Chris's number.

Chris and Elena pulled out of the junkyard when the phone rang. Chris looked at the number and didn't recognize it. He paused, and then answered.

"Yes?" he said.

"Listen, motherfucker. Give me the bitch and I'll forget I we ever talked."

"Who is this?" said Chris. "You got the wrong number, dude."

"This ain't no wrong number. I know you are. Christopher Wolfe."

This sent a mild shock wave through Chris. Who the hell was this, and how did he know his name, and that he had Elena? He felt exposed, naked.

"What do you want?"

"Just give me the ho. Give me the ho and you walk. Plain and simple," said Lincoln. "Otherwise, man. Otherwise I will fuck you up so nasty you will never know what hit you."

Chris remembered the newscast with the Mayor. "You know what?" said Chris. "I know who you are too, asshole. Just saw you on TV with the Mayor."

Lincoln paused. "Give me the ho. You don't know who you're dealing with."

"Oh yes I do," said Chris. "I'm dealing with you, punk."

"I can make it worth your while," said Lincoln.

"How's that?"

"We could maybe work out a little deal. Cash transaction."

"How much?"

"We can figure that out," said Lincoln. "Meet me in front of the party store. You know the one. Right across the street from where you live."

"I got a better idea," said Chris.

"What's that?" said Lincoln.

"Go fuck yourself."

* *

Chris and Elena passed by the apartment and Lincoln's black Tahoe, turned right on Kirby and took Woodward toward I-94 and the airport. He dialed Vlad's number.

"I have your dope," said Chris.

Vlad was silent on the other end.

"I'll make a deal with you," said Chris.

"Deal? What deal would that be?"

"You keep your dope. I'll give it back to you. I keep the girl," said Chris. "Meet me at JetView Parking. I'll be there in a half an hour."

Chris snapped the phone shut right at the entrance to I-94 West toward Chicago and the airport.

* *

Chris stopped in front of the International Terminal.

"Buy some clothes," he said. "And buy a carry on. Put the clothes in it. The money and diamonds should be okay in the checked bag." He pulled her over and kissed her. "This is your best shot. Go. There isn't much time."

Elena held Chris and wouldn't let go. "I love you," she said. "It will work for us. We can live in Florida. Like you said. You, me, and Sanja. I will come back." Elena started crying.

"Call me when you get things settled," said Chris. "Go."

"You saved my life," said Elena. She got out of the car and walked through the terminal door. Chris watched until she was out of sight.

* *

Chris pulled into JetView parking, took the automatic ticket and looked for Vlad's CTS. He drove through the Byzantine rows, and finally saw Vlad. He pulled his gun from his jacket. Vlad sat with the windows up, Glock in his lap.

Chris pulled along side Vlad, the cars facing opposite directions, driver's side windows parallel. Chris rolled down the window. Vlad rolled down his.

"Do you have my property?" said Vlad.

"Yes I do," said Chris. "It's yours. I don't want it. Just leave Elena alone is all I ask," said Chris.

"You do not understand," said Vlad. This is not how the system works. We shook hands. It's your honor." Vlad laughed. "You try to bargain? Make demands? With something that you stole from me?"

"If that's the way you see it, then yeah," said Chris.

Vlad looked at Chris and picked up the Glock. "I liked you," he said. "I thought you were honorable. We could have done great things together. How unfortunate."

Vlad's arm whipped out the open window. He pointed the Glock at Chris and fired. Before Chris could react the world went bright white, then black forever. He slumped to the right over the console, blood seeping from his head onto the passenger's seat.

Vlad got out of the CTS and looked in the window. The heroin was in the back seat. He opened the door, reached in the back, being careful not to get any blood on his silver track suit.

Vlad pulled out of the JetView lot and turned right on Middlebelt Road, away from the airport.

The tiny but powerful transponder broadcast a homing signal as Vlad headed east on I-94.

CHAPTER 37

The Takedown

Vlad drove on I-94 and got off at Woodward. He dialed Lincoln's number. Time to cut losses and eliminate loose ends. And Lincoln was a big loose end. So was Alanzo.

"First, get in touch with our friend," said Vlad. "We have some problems. I just eliminated one of them." He turned onto I-375 toward the River. "We need to make a new deal. I have the product with me," he said. "And second, where are Elena and Miri?"

"I'll get back with you on that one," said Lincoln. "First things first. Let me call Alanzo. I'll call you in fifteen minutes."

Lincoln thought about how he was going to approach Vlad about the whores. Especially the dead one.

* *

"It's a long story," said Lincoln to Alanzo. "Long and short of it, someone stole our shit, but we got it back."

"Man," said Alanzo. "You incompetent or what? How you let someone steal your shit?" he said. "It ain't just yours, it's mine too."

"It's all under control," said Lincoln.

"Gonna cost you," said Alanzo. "Cash money. Now I got all the risk."

"That shouldn't be a problem," said Lincoln.

Alanzo lay back and took a hit from a large blunt. These dudes must be in some kind of shit.

"Tell you what," said Alanzo. "Give me three twenty five along with the shit and we're good."

"Vlad's got it, but I got a better deal for you."

"What's that?" said Alanzo.

"Vlad's got the shit himself. We take Vlad out, and we go get it. All of it. You keep the shit and the money. I just want to get separated from this all this."

Alanzo thought about it. "Sounds reasonable."

"Come packed. I'll call you back. Later, dog."

"Adios," said Alanzo, terminating the call.

* *

Peabody and Washington picked up the transducer signal and followed Vlad to the Roostertail. They saw the CTS parked near the front door. Exposed on the wide open, abandoned spaces on Marquette Drive, Washington turned around and slowly drove the other way.

"Just make sure that signal stays strong," said Peabody.

* *

Vlad sat inside facing the channel and drank a vodka and tonic, thinking of Albania. It was time to go back for a while, let things around here cool. With a little luck he could take both of these budallas out at the same time. He was looking at the empty slips across the street at the Detroit Yacht Club when his phone rang.

"How far are you from Atwater and St. Aubin?" said Lincoln.

"Just a few blocks," said Vlad.

"Our friend will meet us there in a half an hour. Near the old Globe warehouse."

* *

Lincoln got there first, stopped near the derelict Globe Trading Company building and turned off the Tahoe's lights. Alanzo swung around the corner in his Land Cruiser and did the same. Lincoln got out of the Tahoe and walked to the Land Cruiser and got in. An Uzi sat on Alanzo's lap.

"Where the fuck is your friend?" said Alanzo.

"He'll be here," said Lincoln.

A set of headlights turned the corner.

Seeing Lincoln and Alanzo both in the Land Cruiser, Vlad pulled along the driver's side. Might make it easier, killing both with just a few shots. He rolled down the window and looked up at Alanzo.

Alanzo rolled down his window. "Why the fuck do you want to dump the junk in such a hurry? Now I take all the fuckin' risk." Alanzo stared at Vlad. "You got the junk and the money?"

"Money?" said Vlad. "What money?"

Lincoln looked straight ahead as Vlad pulled his Glock and shot Alanzo in the head, twice. Alanzo bounced back and forth in the driver's seat, momentarily hitting the horn.

"What the fuck are you doing?" yelled Lincoln.

Vlad got out of the car. Lincoln slammed the

shifter into drive and the Land Cruiser crept forward. He tried ducking as far as he could beside Alanzo, slumped dead against the wheel. Lincoln pushed down on Alanzo's leg, hitting the accelerator and reached for the Uzi. The Land Cruiser surged forward. Vlad ran and held on to the steering wheel. He shot down at Lincoln, drilling him in the neck and chest. Lincoln gasped, his mouth moving like a fish out of water. Vlad shot again hitting Lincoln right above his left ear, spraying the passenger's window with red mist.

Peabody and Washington saw the last shot being fired. The Land Cruiser slowed and rolled along the open field parallel to Atwater on the left and the abandoned row of buildings on the right.

"Move!" said Peabody and Washington gunned the engine and raced across the field after Vlad, just missing the Land Cruiser. Washington pulled his weapon. Vlad turned and fired. Peabody saw the orange muzzle flash and pop pop pop the windshield spider webbed around three bullet holes, one bullet hitting Washington in the shoulder.

"Shit," cried Washington, stung by the sudden pain.

Peabody opened the door. Vlad fired three more shots, pinging the door twice. One bullet tore through Peabody's ear, stunning her. Vlad stood and aimed. Peabody knelt and fired, hitting Vlad in the chest with two clean, well placed shots.

Vlad dropped to his knees and raised the Glock. Peabody rolled off three more rounds hitting Vlad in the top of the head, skull fragments flying. Vlad dropped face first into the dirt.

Peabody, blood gushing from what remained

of her ear looked at Washington. "Hang in there,"
she said. "Just hang with me."

CHAPTER 38

Sami and the Field

"Sanja," said Milos. "Hide in here. This is not a game. You must stay in here and not say a word." Sanja hid in a small broom closet at the back of the kitchen. "No matter who you hear you stay here until I come and get you. Promise?"

"Promise, Papa," said Sanja, peering out from between two brooms.

"That's good girl. I will be back soon."

* *

Milos sat in the dining room holding the double barrel shotgun when Sami's Mercedes rose over the hill and pulled in front of the cottage. He got out, knocked on the door, and when no one answered walked in. He turned the corner from the main room to the tiny dining area. Milos steadied the shotgun and pointed it at Sami's head.

"What is this?" said Sami, looking down the barrel. "What are you doing? Are you crazy?"

"Crazy to have trusted you with my daughter," said Milos, his finger tightening on the trigger.

Sami opened his mouth to say something, then stopped and hung his head. "Where is Rada?"

"Gone. I will kill her if she comes back," said Milos.

"What? Where will she go?"

"That is not my concern," said Milos. He hefted the shotgun. "Now turn around. Go. Out the front door."

"You aren't going to shoot me, are you?"

"Move," said Milos.

Sami turned and Milos nudged him with the shotgun.

"It was just a business decision, for a debt I owed," said Sami. "It was nothing to do with you, or her. It was just business." Sami walked out the front door followed closely by Milos, who held the shotgun a few feet from the back of Sami's head.

"Turn toward the field," said Milos.

Sami stopped. "The field?" he said.

"Go," said Milos. "Or would you rather face this?" Milos motioned with the shotgun.

"Think about this," said Sami. "I have friends. In high places. You do something to me, something happens to you."

"Where are they now to help you?" said Milos. "Now walk. With your hands up."

Sami turned and started walking in the direction of the open field. "I can make you very rich."

"Rich how? By selling daughters? Mothers? Children? Rich how?" said Milos, his arms feeling the weight of the shotgun. He suppressed a cough.

Sami stopped at the edge of the field. The field, filled with small anti-personnel mines left from the war, was flat and grown over with short grass and tall weeds.

"Walk."

"You really are crazy," said Sami. "The mines."

"Walk."

Sami took two steps forward into the field then turned and rushed at Milos.

"I'll kill you, you stupid fool," he said.

Milos took careful aim and fired, taking off Sami's right hand. Sami dropped to his knees and screamed.

"Get up and walk," said Milos. "Take your chances with the mines. If you make it across, you are free to go. I will not bother you," he said. "If you stay, I will take your head off." Milos aimed the shotgun at Sami's head.

Sami stood on his feet unsteadily, turned and started walking through the field, holding his arm to stop the bleeding.

"I will come back and kill you, I swear," he said, looking toward the end of the field, then down before taking each step.

Sami got fifteen paces and thought he might have a chance of making it to the other side when he heard a small click.

The anti-personnel mine was especially vicious, filled with ball bearings and razor shards. It ripped off Sami's left leg above the knee, destroying his groin and shredding his inner thigh. He dropped screaming to the ground. He lay in a fetal position for a moment then crawled forward. His left elbow triggered another mine near his head.

Milos watched smoke rise from what remained of Sami's body. He lowered the shotgun and walked back to the cottage.

CHAPTER 39

At the Station

Milos took Sanja into the village, passing the Wolf's Head tavern. He wanted to go inside, have a couple of stiff ones, but not with Sanja. How many pleasant hours had he spent in there? Especially in his younger days. He stopped and looked in the wood framed front window. The bartender saw Milos, put down the towel he wiped glasses with and waved, motioning for Milos to come inside. Milos looked down at Sanja, opened the door and walked in.

"Milos," said the bartender. "I have not seen you in ages. I was going to come out and see you today."

"Why?" Milos felt a sense of dread. Had Rada come here?

"There was a call for you."

"A call?"

"Yes. From your daughter. She said this was the only place she knew to call and get word to you. She said to tell you she is arriving tomorrow. Twelve o'clock. At the train station."

Milos squeezed Sanja's hand. Over and over again.

* *

Elena, exhausted from the flights from Detroit to Athens to Tirana fell asleep on the train. The ride from Rinas International went by surprisingly fast. The train slowed and she woke. She gazed out the window. Winter would set in soon. Most of the leaves had fallen and the trees were bare. One thing she noticed after landing in Tirana. The birds were still here, still singing. Elena couldn't remember the last time she listened to birds sing.

The train slowed and Elena jumped to her feet, straining to see the platform from the window. She rushed down the aisle and walked off the car, looked around and saw them, Milos standing with Sanja. Sanja smiled and waved. Elena rushed to them, dropped her bags and held Sanja with her eyes closed for a very long time.

* *

Two days later in the village, Elena stood in the phone booth holding Sanja's hand and dialed Chris's number.

No one answered.

THE END

RECKONING IN ESCOBARA

If you liked this book, chances out you'll like the sequel:

Reckoning in Escobara
by
John Silver

After taking down Vlad Dragovic in Detroit, Ann Peabody quits the DEA and heads to Mexico to investigate and avenge the murder of her brother Jason Peabody, a U.S. Border Patrol agent. The trail leads to Escobara, a suburb of drug cartel controlled Juarez. Peabody becomes a bodyguard and security consultant to Olga Espinosa, the newly elected Mayor of Escobara, and works with Olga and her brother Manuel to rid Escobara of the drug trade and gangs. Ex-DPD Inspector Freeman Washington shows up to help Peabody out.

Along with the multiple, horrific drug-related slayings a serial killer is on the loose around Escobara, and he's *prolific*. Peabody discovers that Jason was killed elsewhere before being found on the Texas-Juarez border. Why? Was he connected to the drug trade, or worse, the serial killer?

...then there's the CIA...

Stand tall with Ann Peabody and Freeman Washington on the vicious streets of Escobara as they build a force to protect the people, unravel the mystery of Jason's murder and uncover the rabid serial killer in RECKONING IN ESCOBARA.

Here's the first chapter:

Chapter 1

Near Escobara, Mexico, Two Years Ago

The pickup truck pulled off the dirt road, drove across the flat earth then eased down an embankment and out of sight. Jason Peabody put the truck in park and killed the ignition and headlights. He looked at the radio clock display. Juanita put her hand on his leg, moved closer and Jason put his arm around her. They sat motionless, looking at the moonlit desert.

"You know I have to get back," said Jason.

Juanita pressed against him. "So soon?"

"What do you mean, so soon? It's almost midnight. I have to report in early tomorrow."

"I bet I can get you to stay." Juanita flipped over and wrapped herself around him, her back pushing against the steering wheel. She was warm, her body heat a haven in the cool desert air. "I'll show you," she said. "Get the blanket. Let's go in the back."

Jason looked up at Juanita and smiled. He spoke to her in Spanish. "Why do you always do this to me?" He glanced at the clock, then said, "What the hell. Should be an easy shift tomorrow. It's Sunday." Juanita hugged him and he kissed the little bluebird tattoo on her shoulder.

Jason's Spanish wasn't the best, but he was learning above what was taught at the Border Patrol Academy. An eight-week language training program taught him the basics but was focused on law enforcement tasks and how to solicit information from detainees and illegals. He learned some slang, and he tried to use it, but the words he chose were usually out of context or made no sense. That always made Juanita laugh.

She slid off Jason. He grabbed a green army surplus blanket from the rear jump seat, opened the door and stepped out into the night. He took a deep breath and felt the cool desert air fill his lungs. Jason stood for a moment, letting his eyes adjust to the dark, then opened the tailgate and spread the blanket. Juanita got out of the truck and Jason helped her into the pickup bed. She laughed and started taking off her top.

"It's cold out here," she said. "Hurry up."

Jason hopped into the bed and slipped on the blanket.

"What's the matter?" said Juanita. "Do I make you nervous?"

"Nervous, no. Turned on, yes." He dropped down on his hands and knees and crawled slowly toward Juanita, like a cat. "Here I come."

This gave Juanita a little shiver. "Don't do that. It scares me."

"I'm coming to get you," said Jason.

Juanita curled up and wrapped her arms around her bare legs. "Don't," she said, her voice rising and falling.

Jason stopped crawling and cocked his head.

"Hear that?"

Juanita looked at him. "No. Quit messing around and come here."

"Shhh. Listen," said Jason. He stood up and looked toward the embankment.

They heard a motor and saw headlights over the crest of the hill. Jason and Juanita looked at each other.

"Who's that?" whispered Juanita.

"Don't know. Looks like a truck or SUV." Jason put his index finger to his lips. "Quiet."

A door opened and someone stepped out of the vehicle. The sound carried in the dense air. Jason and Juanita heard a rough, sliding noise, like sandpaper over wood, canvass over metal. Then *clump-* something heavy hitting the ground. They heard it again. And again.

"What's going on?" said Juanita.

"Shhh. Get down."

Jason and Juanita heard the *shloop* of a metal shovel pitching into dirt and rock, then dirt being thrown and hitting the ground.

"Stay down," said Jason, motioning with his palms. "I'm going to take a look."

Juanita clung to him. "No. Stay here with me. Maybe they'll go away."

"And maybe they won't. I don't want to take any chances. Sounds like only one person, could be a narco. I need to get my gun. And a flashlight."

"Hurry back," said Juanita. "I'm scared."

The digging stopped. Jason pulled away from Juanita and slid over the side of the truck, careful not to make any noise. He crouched down, walked to the driver's side door and reached in the window for his Glock G2. He picked up the Glock and felt for the flashlight. Jason pulled out from the open window, turned, and glimpsed the metal shovel blade before it hit the side of his head, a flash originating on a distant horizon then filling his internal field of vision. The taste in his mouth was metallic. He swooned and dropped the flashlight, but still held the Glock in his right hand.

The man holding the shovel looked at Juanita.

She screamed and saw the shovel blade swing again and hit Jason in the back of the head. Jason fell, his eyes lifeless and mouth open. Juanita scrambled down the tailgate and ran into the desert, her bare feet cut from brush and rocks with every stride.

The man took the Glock from Jason's hand and looked it over. He flipped off the safety, aimed at Juanita and fired. She lurched forward, her eyes bulging from the shock of impact. She fell face forward into the hard-packed earth. The man stood and watched Juanita for a moment, then turned and looked at Jason. He shot Jason in the back and in the side of the head, watching his body bounce slightly with each shot.

He strolled over to Juanita and dragged her up and over the hill and placed her next to three dead, naked women lying in a half dug shallow grave. Each woman had an X carved into their abdomens. He pulled out a small digital camera and snapped a couple of pictures. He took an extra shot of Juanita and her bluebird tattoo. The flash from the camera cut through the dark like lightning. He buried Juanita last...

...he waited until dark before loading the three dead females in the back of the SUV. The naked bodies were wrapped in blankets bound by gray duct tape. The women looked alike. They could have been cousins, even sisters. That's the way he liked them, the whores, the putas de meirda he attracted. Thin, shapely, good looking, using female charms and the promise of sex to get men to make fools of themselves. Holding their power over them to gain control and take their money.

Not these bitches. Not so good looking now, the first being dead five days and the last two days. The smell seeped through the blankets. They were whores, evil sluts who deserved death. It gave him immeasurable pleasure carving an X in their stomachs.

They were so easy to find. Go to any bar or club in Juarez and take your pick. He liked the ones who were haughty and full of themselves. The ones that constantly checked their faces in makeup mirrors. The gold diggers, the aprovechadoras.

He dressed well, but not like a flashy narco, more reserved, and got their attention with his casual, confident way. He made eye contact, smiled and they came to him. If they asked him if he was a dealer he always said no. He told them he was a doctor, lawyer, architect, independently wealthy, or that he inherited money. He flashed cash, but subtly. It was best to be modest, but casually mention a car collection, or maybe a yacht on the Gulf and a gated hacienda. Just give them an inkling of wealth and they drooled like dogs.

This little taste of real money unleashed a torrent of interest and questions. He saw it in their faces and personalities. The slightest hint of money and they hung on every word, laughed at every stupid joke. Bitches. Whores.

It was easy to get them to leave with him after a couple of drinks. He had a rule if he had doubts about killing them. If they touched him, they died. Some were subtle and deceptively innocent, like holding his hand and squeezing it after he said something. Some were less subtle, touching a foot against his and leaving it there. Some were bold, running a hand up his inner thigh…whores…

…The man tossed the shovel into his truck and loaded Jason's body in the back of the pickup, covering it with the green blanket. He got in Jason's truck, started it and drove toward the Juarez-El Paso border. A short way from the border, on the western edge near the base of the mountains, the man pulled onto Nadadores Street and stopped at the dead end near the storage yard. He pulled Jason's body from the back of the pickup and placed him next to the cab on the driver's side, leaving the door open. He rifled through Jason's pockets and the pickup cab. He took Jason's Glock, wallet, badge, watch, and an old 1923 Peace silver dollar that was in Jason's pocket. He rubbed the coin between his fingers and took a final glance at Jason. Satisfied it looked like an ambush or robbery, he turned and walked toward Escobara.

ABOUT THE AUTHOR

John Silver's hard edged thrillers leave you wanting more. Reader comments for the debut thriller **The System – A Detroit Story** range from "this is one entertaining book" to "a story that truly pulls the reader in and delivers a wild ride" to "I think that anyone who enjoys a well written crime novel…will enjoy The System."

Following **The System - A Detroit Story-** is the high impact **Reckoning in Escobara**. Reader comments for **Reckoning in Escobara** are "this is one of the best books ever" and "this is a must read, for sure!!!".

You may also like the historical thriller **Thomas Edison: RESURRECTOR**. Comments for **Thomas Edison: RESURRECTOR** include "I absolutely loved this book" and "I hope to see MANY more from this author."

Visit http://johnsilverbooks.com for details.